NOAH McNICHOL and the BACKSTAGE GHOST

NOAH McNICHOL
and the
BACKSTAGE GHOST

by Martha Freeman

A Paula Wiseman Book
Simon & Schuster Books for Young Readers
NEW YORK   LONDON   TORONTO   SYDNEY   NEW DELHI

SIMON & SCHUSTER BOOKS FOR YOUNG READERS
An imprint of Simon & Schuster Children's Publishing Division
1230 Avenue of the Americas, New York, New York 10020

For information about special discounts for bulk purchases,
please contact Simon & Schuster Special Sales at 1-866-506-1949 or
business@simonandschuster.com.
The Simon & Schuster Speakers Bureau can bring authors to your live event. For more
information or to book an event, contact
the Simon & Schuster Speakers Bureau at 1-866-248-3049
or visit our website at www.simonspeakers.com.
Interior design by Hilary Zarycky
The text for this book was set in ITC New Baskerville
Manufactured in the United States of America
1220 FFG
First Edition
2 4 6 8 10 9 7 5 3 1

Library of Congress Cataloging-in-Publication data
Names: Freeman, Martha, 1956–author.
Title: Noah McNichol and the backstage ghost / by Martha Freeman.
Description: First edition. | New York : Simon & Schuster Books for Young Readers,
[2021] | "A Paula Wiseman Book." | Audience: Ages 8–12. | Audience: Grades 4–6. |
Summary: After their director breaks her leg, the cast of a sixth-grade play is delighted
with volunteer director Mike, but eleven-year-old Noah McNichol has reason to believe
Mike is a ghost.
Identifiers: LCCN 2020030025 (print) | LCCN 2020030026 (ebook) |
ISBN 9781534462908 (hardcover) | ISBN 9781534462953 (ebook)
Subjects: CYAC: Theater—Fiction. | Ghosts—Fiction. | Middle schools—Fiction. |
Schools—Fiction. | Fathers and sons—Fiction.
Classification: LCC PZ7.F87496 No 2021 (print) | LCC PZ7.F87496 (ebook) | DDC
[Fic]—dc23
LC record available at https://lccn.loc.gov/2020030025
LC ebook record available at https://lccn.loc.gov/2020030026

For drama teacher extraordinaire Samantha Howard,
who gave me the idea, and her family
—M. F.

Meet the Plattsfield-Winklebottom Memorial Sixth-Grade Players

Noah McNichol (our hero): Born in New York City, Noah moved with his parents to Plattsfield when he was seven years old. While Noah has been a theater fan since he was old enough to say "Encore," *Hamlet* marks his debut performance.

Clive Desmond (Noah's best friend): Inspired by big sister, Gillian, who starred as Lady Macbeth in a previous Sixth-Grade Play, Clive gave up baseball to take to the boards. Clive was born in Plattsfield, where his family has maintained an apple orchard since 1942.

Emma Jessel (the villain): The only daughter of two very successful lawyers, Emma has a big personality perfectly suited to a big part. Emma's family have been proud residents of New York state since shortly after the Revolutionary War.

Madeline Howard (Emma's best friend): A self-professed theater geek, Madeline reads plays for fun and attends live performances as parents and time permit. Previous roles include Sprinkle Doughnut in the kindergarten pageant, Reluctant Child in a commercial for Your Local Plattsfield Subaru Dealership, and Crying Girl in Santa's Lap in the West Chazy Players production of *A Christmas Story*.

Fuli Tenzing (player): A serious reader and lifelong movie fan, Fuli makes her theatrical debut in the Plattsfield-Winklebottom Memorial Sixth-Grade Play. When she is not studying or reading for pleasure, Fuli can be found helping out at her family's popular downtown restaurant, Himalaya, which has the best dumplings in town.

Brianna Larkin (player): Brianna's self-admitted stage fright is no match for her passion for theater. Her large family includes three older brothers, all of them standout athletes at Plattsfield-Winklebottom Memorial.

Marley Jacobs (player): A Plattsfield native, Marley is the second in her family to take on the Sixth-Grade

Play. Older brother Charles served as stage manager for *The Tempest* several seasons back. Marley is known as a good student, a good friend, and an all-round good kid.

Diego Arcati (player): Diego's recent pursuits include chess club, canoe club, and lacrosse, none of which proved to be the right fit for his energy and offbeat sense of humor. Along with his parents, his teachers are grateful that *Hamlet* has at least kept him busy.

Sarah Monti (player): While the Sixth-Grade Play marks her theatrical debut, Sarah is a seasoned veteran of numerous performances with the Holy Redeemer Catholic Church's bell choir.

Eddie Muir (player): A standout at basketball and cross-country, Eddie is the second generation of his family to appear in the Sixth-Grade Play, his mother having played Mercutio in *Romeo and Juliet*.

Lila Moseley (player): Along with Eddie, Lila is a second-generation Sixth-Grade Player. Her mother, Jeanene, played the title role in *Othello*.

Mia Duffy (stage manager): Mia would like to thank her parents, Annamarie and William Duffy IV, for endowing her with a skill set uniquely suited to management.

Justin Ferri (lights and sound): Bummed when he sprained his shoulder and couldn't play baseball, Justin—a Plattsfield native—agreed to do Coach Fig a favor and help out with the Sixth-Grade Play.

CHAPTER ONE

Monday, Rehearsal Week One, 46 Days till Performance

Miss Magnus went to New York City over spring break to see shows and was crossing Broadway, not even jaywalking, when a taxi hit her and broke her leg in three places, and that's how it started.

Miss Magnus had been teaching at Plattsfield-Winklebottom Memorial Elementary for twenty-five years and had so many sick days saved she didn't have to come back to school till fall, so she didn't. Instead, she sat home with her leg propped up and read poetry to her elderly chihuahua.

At least, that's what my mom heard at Sal's, the mini-mart close to our house, the store we go to if we don't need anything unusual, like matzoh for my dad's favorite weekend breakfast, matzoh brie, which is like scrambled eggs with crackers, only it tastes better than that sounds.

1

"It's pretty funny that our director broke her leg—get it? Break a leg?" Clive said after school that Monday. We were walking from the school's main building to the auditorium next door.

"Not funny exactly. I bet it hurt. But yeah, I get it," I said. *Break a leg!* is what you say to actors when what you mean is *Have a good show!* because if you say something positive, it's bad luck. Theater people think everything is bad luck.

"So without Miss Magnus, who will be in charge?" Clive asked.

"I guess we'll see when we open the door to the auditorium. Can you wait that long?" I said.

"Hey—snark alert," Clive said. "I was merely asking."

"Sorry. I'm worried is all. I have a bad feeling that without Miss Magnus, the grown-ups will mess this up."

"Mess up your chance to be a star?" Clive said.

"You got it." By now we were climbing the steps. "Broadway! Hollywood! My ticket out of this backwater!"

"You're strange, Noah," Clive said.

"What do you expect? I'm a sixth-grade boy trying out for Shakespeare. You're strange too."

"I know, but don't tell my mom," Clive said. "She's not-so-secretly hoping I won't get a part so I can play baseball."

"Ha! You're a dude and you can read. You will definitely get a part."

In the lobby, Clive pointed to a poster on the wall by the box office:

PLATTSFIELD-WINKLEBOTTOM MEMORIAL SIXTH-GRADE PLAYERS PRESENT WILLIAM SHAKESPEARE'S *HAMLET*, THE TALE OF A GRITTY PRINCE WHO LEARNS TO BE PATIENT! ONE NIGHT ONLY: FRIDAY, MAY 8!

The Plattsfield-Winklebottom Memorial Auditorium, the aud, is old-fashioned and massive and fancy. Now, with Clive behind me, I pushed open the heavy door that led from the lobby to the house. Before us, down the long aisle, was the stage, curtain closed, looking small and far away. Right and left of the aisle were rows and rows of seats, enough to hold grandparents, aunts, uncles, cousins, neighbors— practically the whole town of Plattsfield.

I was in second grade the first time I walked into the aud, probably for a presentation on playground safety or the alphabet from *A* to *Z*. Back then, I was a very small person in a very large space. The stage might as well have been in Canada. The ceiling

3

seemed as distant as the sky. I can't describe how it made me feel exactly, but the feeling was strong. I don't mean I felt scared or puny or unimportant, which would have made sense. Instead, it was more like the opposite, as if I had the power to expand, grow big enough to fill the emptiness.

So even before I ever saw a play in it, I loved the aud for the feeling I got when I was there. Then, the same year, I think, my parents took me to the sixth-grade play, and even though I didn't understand the story exactly, and even though I had to pee really bad, I thought that was great too. The actors were only sixth graders, same as I am now, but when they put on costumes and makeup and spoke strange, beautiful words, they became something else: the characters they were playing.

That day, Clive and I ran down the aisle. I think he was excited, too, even though, cool as he is, he never would've admitted it. Since the house lights were up, we could see that already around twenty kids were clustered in the seats closest to the stage. Most of them I'd known since my family moved to town almost five years ago. Plattsfield, New York, is not very big.

"I don't see a teacher," Clive said. "Maybe Mrs.

Winklebottom couldn't find anybody. I heard no one wants to do it. They've all got too many kids and extra jobs."

Squeals and high fives—"Hey!" "Hey!" "Hello!" I mean, all of us had seen each other, like, half an hour before, but we did the long-lost friend thing anyway. Drama geeks, right?

And with or without a director, we were excited to be getting started.

I guess because of Mrs. Winklebottom—Mrs. Winklebottom and her money—the Plattsfield-Winklebottom Memorial Sixth-Grade Play is a big deal. I'm going to bet everyone in the auditorium that day went to it with their families every year. Clive's big sister, Gillian, had acted in it when we were in third grade. Lila Moseley's and Eddie Muir's moms had been in it when they were kids. Maybe other kids' parents had too.

Not my parents, though. My family's not from here, and I wasn't born here. Around Plattsfield, that makes me strange, an outsider.

Meanwhile, everybody at rehearsal was talking about who the new director would be.

"Mrs. Winklebottom is going to direct us *herself*. I have it on *good authority*," said Emma Jessel.

"What does that even mean—*good authority?*" asked Sarah Monti.

Emma rolled her eyes the way she does. "Well, if *you* don't know, far be it from *me* to tell you." Emma was standing right next to me. Her loud voice rang in my ear, and I took a step away.

"She means she heard it somewhere," Clive told Sarah. Clive, even if he called me a snark, is actually one of the nicer people in sixth grade.

"Well, so what? Because I heard—on *authority*—that Mr. Irving is going to do it, only he'll have to bring his new baby, so half the time he'll be"—Sarah made a face—"*changing diapers.*"

Brianna Larkin said, "This is going to be a disaster."

Madeline Howard said, "I love babies."

Diego Arcati said, "You guys! You guys! *I* know—"

But whatever he knew, we didn't find out. From onstage came the hissing of the ropes raising the curtain, and—like a well-trained audience—we went silent. There must've been someone in the tech booth because—*buzz*—the stage lights came up, and there stood Mrs. Winklebottom herself.

"*See?*" Emma said.

"*Shhhh!*" everybody told her.

"Greetings, sixth graders!" Mrs. Winklebottom

6

is the kind of person you can't believe was ever young. You can't believe she will ever die. She is and always was Mrs. Winklebottom. She wears and always wore either a red, a purple, or a blue dress—red that day—matching jewels in her ears, and heeled, uncomfortable-looking shoes with buckles.

"By now you have all heard the unfortunate news about dear Miss Magnus's encounter with a taxi," Mrs. Winklebottom continued. "But, as the Bard said, fear not! I have arranged for someone else to take over directing duties for this year's production. With your permission, I would like to introduce your new director now."

Well-trained audience, right? We kids clapped and whistled. From the wings strolled Mr. Nate Newton, the gym teacher, wearing headphones, muttering and looking into the great faraway.

In other words, he was on his phone.

"*Coach Fig!*" Diego hollered.

"Hello? What was that?" Mrs. Winklebottom squinted.

We sat in silence, stunned silence I mean. Mr. Newton—known as Coach Fig—is one of those bulgy kind of guys, with some bulges being muscle and others probably fat. He's a good guy, popular, with six kids of his own he talks about all the time. Besides knowing the rules to every sport, he doesn't blame you for being a klutz, doesn't favor the superstar athletes either.

But did he know downstage from upstage? Unlikely.

"Hang on a mo, so sorry," he said to whoever he had on the phone. Then he looked around, oriented himself in real life. "Hey, you guys. Hey, Mrs. Winklebottom. This *Hamlet* play is gonna be great, you know what? I mean, we are gonna *dominate!*"

"Excuse me! Mrs. Winklebottom?"

"Is that Mia Duffy addressing me?" Mrs. Winklebottom said. "With the lights, you're a bit of a blur."

"Mrs. Winklebottom," said Mia, "first, can I just say thank you for all you've done for the performing arts?"

"You're quite welcome, I'm sure," Mrs. Winklebottom said. "Now"—she looked at her watch—"if you don't mind, I have—"

"I'm not done," Mia said.

"Oh," said Mrs. Winklebottom.

"What I'd like to know, with all due respect, is this: What exactly is Coach Newton's theatrical background?"

Mia Duffy's family are neighbors of Mrs. Winkle-bottom. They live on the nicest street in Plattsfield, the one that overlooks the lake and has all the big houses, which is why, I'm guessing, she thought she could be rude like that. Usually I think Mia Duffy is a pain, but that day I was grateful.

Mrs. Winklebottom straightened her shoulders and her frown. "Well, Mia, dear, I think I'll allow the coach himself to answer."

Coach Fig had returned to his call, but something alerted him to look up, first at Mrs. Winklebottom, then at us. "I'm just happy to be here," he said. "And I want to thank all the people who made it possible. Now, who else is ready for kickoff?"

"Heck yeah!" said Diego, who has a reputation for being outrageous, mostly meaning he dresses funny. Also he is super enthusiastic. According to Clive, you have to love the kid or else you'd be tempted to punch him.

Mrs. Winklebottom took a deep breath and let it out. "I know we all appreciate Mr. Newton's dedication," she said. "Now on to practical matters. Rehearsal schedules will be available before you leave this afternoon. Scripts will be here tomorrow for pickup so you can study before auditions on

Wednesday. With the time remaining today, perhaps you could warm up with recitations?"

"Recitations," Fig repeated. "Fan-*tas*-tic!"

Blowing two-handed kisses, Mrs. Winklebottom retreated offstage. "*Adieu, adieu, adieu,*" she said, voice fading. "'Remember me-e-e-e!'"

"What was that about?" Clive asked.

"Like we could forget Mrs. W," Emma said.

"It's from the play," Madeline said. "Act one. The sun's about to come up, and the ghost can't be out in daylight. He's telling Hamlet goodbye."

Clive said, "Whoa—you read the play already."

Diego said, "There's a ghost in this play? How cool is that!"

Brianna said, "I hate ghosts. And spiders."

Meanwhile, Mr. Newton called, "Hey, see ya, Mrs. W! And thanks again for that donation. Those old goalposts were hanging by rust and paint."

With Mrs. Winklebottom gone, Fig stowed his phone in a pocket and sat down on the edge of the stage, feet dangling. "So, team, here's the deal," he said. "I don't know jumping jacks about plays, but Mrs. W was in a bind and I offered to help out. Eight weeks, right? So, first things first. Who can explain to me *recitations*?"

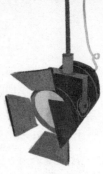

CHAPTER TWO

Four girls raised their hands to answer Fig's question. Diego didn't raise his hand. He just answered: "Stand up and say a poem or something."

"Excellent!" said Fig. "Outstanding! So I'm gonna guess you guys can handle that on your own. Any problems? Shout out and I'm there." With that, he dropped from the stage to the floor of the house, walked back a few rows, and took a seat on the aisle.

"You are supposed to direct us," Mia said.

Fig looked up. "Right, right. I hereby direct you to stand on that stage, speak real loud, and, uh . . . give it all you got for Plattsfield-Winklebottom Memorial!"

Clive looked at me. "This is bad."

"No duh. How much do you know about *Hamlet?*"

"Uh . . . William Shakespeare wrote it a long time ago, and the main character makes a speech that starts 'To be, or not to be,'" he said. "Plus, now I know there's a ghost."

I nodded. "Same. Without a director, we're gonna be up there in front of our parents speaking random speeches we don't understand."

"Maybe not," Clive said. "We got Madeline."

He looked around at her, and then so did I. Till that day I'd always thought of Madeline as kind of an airhead. Now I guessed she was an airhead . . . and a Shakespeare expert.

"But what about the sets and the lights and the crowns and armor and all that?" I said.

Clive was shaking his head. "This is gonna be *bad.*"

Brianna, two seats over, chimed in: "A disaster. And my grandparents are planning to come too . . . all the way from Poughkeepsie!"

"Okay, you guys." While the rest of us had been yakking, Mia had climbed the steps to the stage. "I'll go first. Then Clive, then Lila—"

"Who put you in charge?" Emma asked.

"I put myself," said Mia. "Otherwise we don't do anything, and I, for one, do not have that kind of time. Now listen up." Hands on hips, she looked toward the cheap seats, took a breath, and gave all she had for Plattsfield-Winklebottom Memorial:

"'Twas the night before Christmas, when all through the house . . .'"

Kids sniggered. Kids groaned. But by the time she got to "Ma in her kerchief and I in my cap," we were mostly listening and, speaking for myself at least, trying to think of something to recite.

The Pledge of Allegiance?

"Oh! Susanna"?

Where the Wild Things Are?

The last one, which my mom used to read to me when I was little, gave me an idea. It was a for-real poem, silly but as good as "The Night Before Christmas" any day. Clive got up after Mia, as directed, and recited "Twinkle, Twinkle, Little Star" (groans), then Lila recited "This Little Piggy Went to Market" (more groans).

"Okay, Noah, you're up," said Mia.

"Who? *Moi?*" I said.

Mia gave me a lethal look.

"Okay, okay, I'm ready," I said.

Clive and Lila had walked up onstage a stair at a time—*boring!* I made an entrance, bounced out of my front-row seat, ran three steps, put my palms on the stage, pushed up, somersaulted forward and straightened up, and—*ta-da!*

True, my back was to the audience, but still: It was an entrance.

"No-*AH*! No-*AH*! No-*AH*!" chanted Clive.

I turned around and grinned. "Thank you. Thank you. Thank you very much."

"We're waiting, Noah," Mia said.

I began:

*"You are old, Father William," the young man
said,
"And your hair has become very white;
And yet you incessantly stand on your head—
Do you think, at your age, it is right?"*

*"In my youth," Father William replied to his son,
"I feared it might injure the brain;
But now that I'm perfectly sure I have none,
Why, I do it again and again."*

The poem goes on from there—six more stanzas. In the end, Father William gets annoyed and tells his son,

*"I have answered three questions, and that is
enough,"*

Said his father; "Don't give yourself airs!
Do you think I can listen all day to such stuff?
Be off, or I'll kick you downstairs!"

which, when I was little and my dad read it to me, I thought was the funniest thing in the world.

The Plattsfield-Winklebottom Memorial Sixth-Grade Players thought it was funny too, and I earned a big laugh. But as I was taking my bow (and Mia was saying, "Okay, Noah. You can sit down now"), something strange happened: A breath of cold wind blew through, ruffling papers, mussing hair, raising goose bumps.

We all looked at each other, and Mia said, "Close that door!" and Brianna said, "I don't like this," and Madeline said, "It's a ghost."

Even Coach Fig looked up. "What just happened?"

Nothing, apparently. Everything was soon as before, and Emma got up to recite, and we forgot the wind, and things went back to normal.

That's what we thought anyway.

When everyone had recited, Mia led stretching exercises, and then it was 5:00 p.m. and time to go. Fig told us we were fan-*tas*-tic and—after Mia reminded him—handed out rehearsal schedules.

Clive and I were on our way up the aisle when Fig called us back. "Hey, guys? Do you know anything about turning on this light?" When we turned around, he was standing next to the light he meant—a plain bulb on a pole center stage. It was sort of like a floor lamp. "Mrs. Winklebottom said I was supposed to before I left, but I don't see the switch," he continued.

"That's the ghost light," Clive said.

"Oh yeah, I've heard of that," I said.

Clive shoved me. "You have not."

"So what is it?" Fig asked.

"Every theater has one," Clive said. "Gillian told me. It keeps the ghost company when there's no people around."

"What ghost?" Fig asked.

"Whatever one happens to haunt this theater, I guess," Clive said. "But I don't know how to turn it on."

Then something weird happened. As we watched, the bulb lit all on its own.

"Huh." Fig shook his head and shrugged. "Must be on a timer or something. Anyway, see you Wednesday, guys."

Clive and I walked out of the aud, down the steps, across the courtyard, and over to parent pickup together.

"Do you need a ride?" Clive asked me.

"My dad'll be here in a few," I said.

Some kids climbed on the late bus; the rest got into cars. Soon I was the only kid on the sidewalk. This didn't make me nervous or anything. It was still plenty light, and I was in front of my very own school. Still, I jumped when I heard the voice. It seemed to come out of nowhere.

"Young man? I believe I might be able to help with *Hamlet.*"

CHAPTER THREE

There were three benches on the sidewalk by parent pickup. The voice belonged to a man sitting on the one closest to me. Had he been there when we came out of the auditorium? I hadn't seen him.

He was an older guy, grandpa-age, energetic-looking. His face looked worn but at the same time ready to laugh. His hair was gray and stuck out from under an old-fashioned cloth hat, the kind men wore for work in the photos in your history textbook. His coat was old-fashioned, too, made of brown wool, not down like everyone else's, and it buttoned up the front. On one of the lapels was a tiny gold Star of David pin. It glinted in the light, which is why I noticed it, I guess.

Whoever he was, he must've been Jewish, like me.

"You're staring," the man said.

18

"Sorry!" I said.

"I have some experience in the theater," he went on. "Goes back a ways, but then, so does *Hamlet*. I understand Miss Magnus is unavailable this year, and I'm here to offer my services."

I nodded. I was probably still staring. "You know Miss Magnus?"

"By reputation," he said.

I wasn't sure what that meant, but I nodded again. "Uh . . . help would be great."

Coach Fig hadn't paid attention to a single recitation, had spent the whole afternoon on his phone. One time, still on the phone, he raised his voice and said, "Pink roses and day lilies," like pink roses and day lilies were very important.

What did the P.E. teacher want with pink roses and day lilies?

Anyway, Fig might be a good guy, but he wouldn't be much help with *Hamlet*.

"Excellent," the man said. "As it happens, I have free time at present." Out of his pocket he slid an iPad—I think it was an iPad—a tablet anyway, one with an eerie green glow. The man tapped the screen, glanced at it, looked at me. "I see that auditions are set for Wednesday?"

"That's right . . . but, hey." I glanced over his shoulder. "Is that the rehearsal schedule you've got there? Where did you find it?"

"Inside pocket," he said.

Funny guy, I thought. "The thing is, Mr.—"

"Please call me Mike," he said.

"Mike," I repeated. "And my name's—"

"Noah McNichol."

"Yeah, but how did you—"

"The pleasure is mine," he said.

"Very nice to meet you, too. But, anyway, even if it's a great idea, you can't just show up at our school and volunteer. You have to do paperwork and get clearances and—"

Mike looked puzzled. "Clearances?"

"To show you're not a criminal? You have to go to the office and—" I was going to explain, but then, behind me, I heard a car, and I turned my head, and it was my dad.

"Oh, hey, Mike," I said. "Nice talking, but my ride—" I looked back at the bench.

Mike was gone.

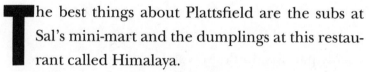

CHAPTER FOUR

The best things about Plattsfield are the subs at Sal's mini-mart and the dumplings at this restaurant called Himalaya.

People don't move to Plattsfield for subs or dumplings, though. They move here, if they do at all, because there are family-size houses with yards available for not much money, because the Adirondack Mountains are a few miles south, because there is a big shining lake surrounded by beaches and rocks and hiking trails, and if you want, you can stick a boat in the water and row to the other side and you will be in Vermont, where there are red barns and spotted cows and cheese.

My family moved to Plattsfield because the parentals got jobs at the college. My dad—his name is Larry—teaches physics, and my mom, Sarah, teaches English.

Plattsfield is okay, but I've never forgiven them for leaving New York City, which is where—as a total real-live theater geek—I was meant to be, walking on concrete with a view of the Statue of Liberty, glittering in the glare of bright lights, navigating among sandwich boards offering cheap bus tours and carts selling hot dogs and caramel nuts.

Only it didn't work out that way.

The parentals rejected all that in favor of a house and zinnias and roomy parking lots with easy access to Target and Walmart and Hannaford.

My parents don't even ski!

Which (after the subs and the dumplings) is another good reason to live in Plattsfield. Skiing is only an hour away in the mountains. Clive and I go most weekends in winter. The parentals don't have a boat on the lake, either, or a dog to frolic in the backyard. All either of them does, as far as I can tell, is work and take care of me and once in a while go to somebody else's house for dinner.

I asked them about this once.

"We like working," my mom said.

"It's interesting," my dad said.

For vacations we visit Florida (my dad's relatives) or California (my mom's).

There's one other thing about Plattsfield, and that's religion, the whole God question. Is God Christian? Is God Jewish? There's this one girl, Fuli, who's also a Sixth-Grade Player. Her family owns the restaurant that makes the dumplings, and I think she might belong to some totally different religion, but it would be rude to ask, wouldn't it?

Anyway, most people in Plattsfield are Christian, and a lot—like Clive—go to Holy Redeemer, which is Catholic. I go there, too, sometimes, with Clive's family, which my parents say helps round out my education. But we aren't Christian at all, we're Jewish, which for us means we celebrate Hanukkah and Passover and we go out for Chinese food on Christmas.

One time I asked my dad how come we don't go to church or temple, either, and he said, "We do. We go to the Church of Family Dinner."

(SCENE: Early evening, the same day. NOAH, DAD, and MOM are seated at the table in the dining room of a comfortable, un-fancy traditional house. The furnishings are simple, far from new, tasteful; framed museum posters hang on the walls. Through the doorway upstage left, the kitchen can be seen. A second doorway, downstage right, leads to the front

hall. NOAH, DAD, and MOM are eating dinner as they talk.)

DAD *(gangly, clean shaven, full head of graying hair)*: The man can't have disappeared, Noah. People don't disappear. It's physically impossible. And I should know. I teach—

NOAH: Physics. I realize, Dad. But I'm telling you—

MOM *(substantial, curly hair that needs a cut, amused eyes)*: Dear? Noah's the only one who was there. Let him tell his story.

DAD: I'm only saying—

(MOM gives him a look.)

DAD: Fine. Sorry. Continue, Noah. The well-dressed gentleman, name of Mike, disappeared from the bench and then what?

NOAH: Then nothing. I got in the car with you, and we drove home.

MOM: Hmm, Noah. Your ending lacks something in the boffo department.

DAD: That's because it's real life, dear, not one of your English assignments.

NOAH: What's "boffo?"

MOM: You know—Wham! Bang! Pow! Either everybody dies in a hail of bullets or the sun rises and kiss-kiss, the pastor pronounces them husband and wife.

NOAH: *Ewww*—mushy-gushy.

DAD: So what's your hypothesis, Noah? Was the guy a specter or what?

MOM: Specter means—

NOAH: Specter means ghost, Mom. I *know*. I've been hanging around professors my whole life. And I haven't formed a hypothesis, Dad. It was merely freaky how he seemed to come and go is all. Plus he knew my name. Plus he had this weird-looking green iPad.

MOM: He knew your name?

DAD: Probably a long-lost relative—like Hamlet's ghost, returned to earth to seek revenge.

NOAH: Revenge for what?

DAD: *That* is the question.

MOM: No, it's not. The question is "To be, or not to be?"

DAD: I defer to the English professor.

NOAH *(looks at each parent)*: I'm lost.

MOM *(looks at NOAH)*: I guess you haven't read the script yet?

NOAH: They aren't passing them out till tomorrow.

DAD: I believe it's widely available on the Internet, possibly on our own bookshelves somewhere.

NOAH: Yeah, this girl Madeline already read it. But

we're doing the No-Trauma Drama edition.

DAD: No-Trauma . . . wha'?

MOM: It's an abbreviated, less bloody version of *Hamlet* written for young people.

DAD: Someone dared to bowdlerize the Bard?

NOAH: Bowdlerize? Bard? Sheesh, parentals, what now?

MOM: A bard is a storyteller. It's another way of saying Shakespeare. "Bowdlerize" means cut out the gruesome parts and the sexy parts.

DAD: Do that to *Hamlet,* and there's not much left.

NOAH: There's sex in *Hamlet?*

DAD: Read it and see.

MOM: Anyway, "To be, or not to be, that is the question" is the start of the most famous soliloquy in the play.

DAD: Do you know what a soliloquy is?

NOAH: No, and don't tell me. "Boffo," "bard," and "bowdlerize" are plenty. Besides, since when are you a theater geek? I thought you hated theater.

DAD: I do not hate theater. I appreciate plays for what they are—entertainment. Just don't fall in love with the whole idea of theater. And don't, whatever you do, try to make a career of it. That will only lead . . . to *heartbreak.*

MOM *(raises eyebrows, looks at DAD)*: For someone who's not a theater fan, you can be quite a drama queen. You know that, right?

DAD: I was going for boffo!

NOAH: What's for dessert?

CHAPTER FIVE

Tuesday, Rehearsal Week One, 45 Days till Performance

There was no rehearsal the next day after school. Instead, we were supposed to pick up our scripts, take them home, and study them.

Clive and I walked over to the aud with Fuli, the girl whose family makes the dumplings, the girl who's unusual like me because she wasn't born in Plattsfield. I came here in second grade. She came here in third. She was born in the country where you go to climb Mount Everest.

In the auditorium lobby, Mrs. Winklebottom was waiting for us behind a table piled with *Hamlet* scripts.

"Welcome! Welcome!" said Mrs. Winklebottom, whose dress that day was purple. "And may I say, it's nice that this year we'll have diversity in our production!"

At first I didn't know what Mrs. Winklebottom

was talking about, but then I realized she meant Fuli and Clive. Practically everybody in Plattsfield is white, but Clive's dad is Black, from Jamaica. Mr. Desmond came here to pick apples a long time ago and wound up marrying his boss's daughter.

"Uh, thanks," Clive said.

"You know, don't you, that color-blind casting is all the rage on Broadway," Mrs. Winklebottom continued. "High time we in Plattsfield embrace it as well."

I'm a white kid myself. Mostly I don't think about that or what color Fuli's skin is or Clive's. I guess that's what the parentals mean when they talk about white privilege. My privilege is not having to think about it.

Anyway, all this with Mrs. Winklebottom felt pretty awkward.

Fuli said, "Very good, Mrs. Winklebottom. I think we each sign this paper and take a script?"

"That's right, my dear. And on the audition sheet here, write which part you're trying out for. Of course, there are only two roles for females, Gertrude and Ophelia, both quite demanding. A lot of the girls will have to play boys. Which role were you thinking of? A gravedigger perhaps?"

"Hamlet," Fuli said.

29

Mrs. Winklebottom laughed.

Fuli didn't.

Mrs. Winklebottom's penciled-on eyebrows shot up. "Well," she said after a pause. "I suppose there's nothing wrong with aiming high. Doesn't Hamlet himself tell us to 'defy augury'? And what about you two?" She looked at Clive and me.

I'd already told Clive I wanted to play Hamlet. But I wasn't going to say that now. "I don't actually know the play very well. I'm going to study it tonight."

Clive didn't answer her. He asked a question. "Where's Coach Newton?"

"He's interviewing a possible assistant," Mrs. Winklebottom said. "I hope it works out. What with the wedding and his teaching duties, Coach does seem overtaxed!"

"Wait—Fig's married already," I said, which I knew because he went to Holy Redeemer, like Clive, and I'd seen him there.

Mrs. Winklebottom frowned. "Fig . . . ?"

"Coach Newton, I mean."

"Oh yes, Coach is married . . . to my stepsister's second-cousin-in-law. Lovely girl, always turning out granola bars for some team or another. But this is someone else's wedding entirely. I believe the happy couple is from Albany, or was it Binghamton? The big city. They're getting married here because our scenery is so very lovely, and Coach Newton is doing the planning. Wedding planning is his 'side gig,' I think he calls it."

Now I got it about the day lilies and the roses. They must be flowers for the wedding.

Clive and I had stuffed our scripts in our backpacks without looking. Fuli was paging through hers. I looked over her shoulder. Double-spaced. Large type. Not that long, luckily. Not that much to memorize.

The three of us said goodbye to Mrs. Winklebottom —"*Adieu! Adieu!*" she replied—pushed open the heavy doors, and went outside.

"Do you really want to play Hamlet?" I asked Fuli. "Or were you messing with Mrs. Winklebottom?"

"Which I could totally understand," Clive said.

"I want to play Hamlet," she said.

"So do I," I said.

"May the best man win," said Clive.

"Man?" Fuli repeated.

Clive shrugged. "The guy's my best friend," he said at the same time Madeline—well-known airhead and Shakespeare expert—came toward us on her way to get her script.

Madeline always looks distracted, like someone with earbuds in, except she doesn't have earbuds in. I think she would have walked by without seeing us if Clive hadn't stopped in front of her and said, "Greetings."

"What?" She stopped, looked at Clive, looked at Fuli, looked at me. "Oh. Hi."

"And what part do you want, Miss Overachiever?" Clive asked.

Madeline looked confused. "Miss . . . ? Oh. Because I read the play, you mean."

"It's cool you read the play," I said. "What's it about, anyway? I mean, besides Hamlet."

"It's like *The Lion King*," Madeline said. "Only the ending's different, and it's in a castle instead of the jungle."

"Cool," I said. "And I suppose you want to play Hamlet, too?"

Madeline shook her head. "Ophelia. She wants to be Hamlet's girlfriend, then Hamlet kills her father and she goes crazy and drowns herself."

Clive scratched his head, looked at me, looked at Madeline. "I don't remember that from *The Lion King*."

"It sounds intense," I said.

Madeline nodded. "The story's intense. In the end, there's swords and blood and poison."

Clive and I looked at each other: "Cool!"

Clive added, "Anyway, not to be insulting, but you don't seem that crazy."

For a heartbeat, Madeline stared. Then she rolled her eyes back in her head, put her arms out in front of her, spun in circles, screamed like a police siren, and *then*—this was the worst part—began to burble in a singsong voice: "'He is dead and gone, lady, he is dead and gone! At his head a grass-green turf, at his heels a stone.'"

Then she stopped stock-still and stared up at Clive.

Personally? I was too freaked out to react, but Fuli applauded and Madeline bowed, and I took a breath and applauded, too. I mean, that had been *amazing*.

Clive was rattled. I could tell. But he acted cool as usual. "I take it back. You are that crazy. Uh . . . were those lines from the play?"

"Act four."

Clive nodded. "I knew that."

Madeline half smiled, looked away, continued up the steps to the aud.

"Freaky, right?" I said to Clive.

He nodded. "Gillian—my sister—she says you gotta watch out for the quiet ones."

We descended the steps, crossed the courtyard. "So, Fuli, how come you want to play Hamlet, anyway?" I asked. "No offense—I mean, you look okay and everything—but you don't exactly look like a prince."

Fuli stopped, straightened her shoulders, tugged her black hair back, and faced me. "What about this? Imagine a crown."

"Maybe," I said. "A short prince."

"So I will be a short prince," Fuli said.

"Pretty confident," Clive said.

Fuli didn't smile often, so when she did—like now—you noticed. "I want to play Hamlet because it is the biggest part, the lead. I want to see if I can do it, test myself. And if I can say something true? From my heart?"

I wasn't sure I wanted to hear it. I didn't know Fuli that well. But Clive said, "Please do."

"I don't want to be only the girl with the dumplings." She grinned when she said it, and I laughed, which seemed to be okay with her. But Clive didn't laugh. He nodded, looked serious.

"Tell me, Noah," Fuli went on. "How will you prepare for the role?"

"Excuse me?" I said.

"There are movies of *Hamlet,* you know? I am going to watch a couple and try to understand the character better. And of course I'll study the script. Hamlet is called 'the melancholy Dane.' I want to understand exactly what makes him sad."

By this time we'd reached the curb at parent pickup, and I noticed the bench where yesterday I'd seen the mysterious Mike. Could he be the assistant Mrs. Winklebottom told us about? Probably not. Probably Fig had recruited some drama student from the college. Probably I would never see Mike again.

Clive's mom was on her way. She was giving Fuli a ride, too. I looked at Fuli and shrugged. "Sounds good, Fuli. Sounds like you gave yourself homework. But just to warn you, I've seen *The Lion King* a bunch of times. *Both* versions."

CHAPTER SIX

I t was four o'clock when I let myself into my house. Since it was Tuesday, Mom and Dad would walk home from the college together around five, and later—around six thirty—we would eat Family Dinner, which in our house is an everyday thing. My parents take turns cooking. We sit in the dining room. I set the table, clear the table, and load the dishwasher.

As a little kid, I thought Family Dinner was normal. When later I realized no other family in the solar system operates like us, I wanted to know how I got so lucky (not!), and the parentals explained that they think it's important to "have a ritual connection each day with those you love best."

If you're wondering, yes, I have pointed out we could ritually connect at Mickey D's or KFC or by eating pizza from Bazzano's in front of the TV—same as other people.

This argument gets me nowhere.

And last year one time, probably in the car, my mom told me something that made me sad. She said when my dad was little, he was always being left with babysitters so his parents could go to parties and plays and whatever, and he didn't want to do the same thing to his kid, to me.

Basically, I am a nice guy. Not as nice as Clive, not as convinced I have a right to take up space in the universe, either, but still . . . nice. And after Mom told me that, I stopped complaining (so much) about Family Dinner.

My only homework that afternoon was geometry. For brainpower, I ate raspberry yogurt and Oreos, which must have worked because, leaning back against the pillows on my bed, notebook on my knees, I got the geometry done in twenty minutes.

After that it was time to read *Hamlet.*

The play is interesting, I guess. Once upon a time in Denmark, there's a prince in a castle haunted by a ghost who claims to be his father, the king, who died not that long before the action begins. Only, according to the ghost, Hamlet's father didn't plain die; he was poisoned by the current king—Hamlet's uncle Claudius, the villain.

So anyway, the ghost tells Hamlet he has to get revenge by killing Claudius and taking the crown for himself.

Meanwhile, there are all these other characters, like Hamlet's mother, Gertrude, who is now married to Claudius (!), and this guy Polonius, who works for the government and makes long speeches and has a beautiful daughter, Ophelia, the one Madeline wanted to play, the one who's all mushy-gushy over Hamlet.

We learned in English that stories have to have conflict. In *Hamlet* the conflict is kind of between Hamlet and Hamlet. In other words, he can't decide what to do.

On the one hand, Hamlet wants to do what his father, the ghost, says because he wants to be a good son and, TBH, he's not crazy about his uncle.

On the other hand, how can Hamlet be sure the ghost really *is* his father? Besides which, is Hamlet really up for killing anybody? Even a villain? Supposedly Hamlet is brave, but in the end he seems to me like more of a thinker type, killing not exactly his style.

I don't want to give away the ending, except to say

that Madeline must have misunderstood something. No poison. No blood. No swords. Ophelia doesn't drown, either. She just goes for a moonlight swim.

Of course, like I explained, the script we had was the No-Trauma Drama version. Maybe the way Shakespeare wrote it was a little different.

(SCENE: Dining room, early evening. NOAH, DAD, and MOM are eating dinner.)

DAD: Are we out of that breakfast cereal I like?

MOM: I didn't notice. Anyway, you can pick some up when you go to the grocery store.

DAD *(puts fork down, shakes head)*: It's your turn to go to the store. I went last time.

MOM *(puts fork down, becoming irritated)*: That's what you always say, dear. But the fact is I was at Sal's—

DAD *(also becoming irritated)*: Sal's does not count as going to the store. Sal's is more like the trading post for gossip—

NOAH: Now, now, parentals. *(He raises a hand for silence.)* "Beware of entrance to a quarrel!"

(MOM and DAD, taken aback, look at each other.)

MOM: Does Polonius say that?

DAD *(nods)*: Part of the advice he gives his son. I had to memorize it back in the day. "But being

in, bear't that the opposed may beware of thee."
That's the next part, right?

NOAH: I think. I'm not sure I get it, though. What's
a bear got to do with it?

DAD: Not that kind of bear. The idea is if you're going
to argue, don't do it halfway. Put some muscle in
it.

MOM (*nodding*): Impressive knowledge, dear. Especially for someone who thinks theater is a phase
you grow out of.

DAD: I never said that.

MOM: You did. About an hour ago. We were walking
by Sal's.

DAD: We should have picked up cereal.

MOM (*ignores DAD, looks at NOAH*): So I take it you
got hold of the *Hamlet* script. What part are you
going to try for?

NOAH: Hamlet.

MOM: Aim high.

NOAH: That's what Mrs. Winklebottom told Fuli.
She's trying out for Hamlet too.

DAD: Fuli . . . she's the one from Nepal?

NOAH: That's it—the country I always forget.

DAD: That restaurant of theirs, they make the *best*
dumplings.

MOM: Are you worried about the competition?

NOAH *(shrugs):* I think I can take her on. She doesn't look very Danish.

MOM *(frowns)*: When it comes to that, Noah, I don't think I've ever seen a Hamlet with curly red hair, either.

NOAH: Red*dish.*

DAD: If the director's doing his job, looks won't have much to do with it. The best actor should get the part, the one who can dig in and inhabit the character, the one who makes the audience care about Hamlet's dilemma.

NOAH: Right? And that settles it. Because you know what, *Grrrrr!*

(MOM and DAD look at each other, look at NOAH.)

NOAH: Lions, get it? Simba? I guess the stories are the same, right? *(sings)* "And I just can't wait to be king!"

CHAPTER SEVEN

Wednesday, Rehearsal Week One, 44 Days till Performance

It's easier to act all confident with your parents at Family Dinner than it is to feel all confident moments before you're going to stand on the stage of a massive, grand, old-fashioned auditorium, with your knees shaking while you recite long words from an old play, which is another way to say that by Wednesday afternoon I felt nervous.

Not that I thought Fuli would beat me out for the part exactly. How could serious, quiet, precise Fuli be a better actor than me, Noah McNichol?

And anyway, like I said, she just doesn't look like Hamlet.

I am skinny with freckles and wavy reddish hair. Not red. Red*dish.* My mom says I'm entering the underfed years and I'll fill out, unless, like my skinny-as-spaghetti uncle Andy, I don't, but that's okay because Uncle Andy has always been catnip with the ladies, and when Mom says that, I shake my head and cover my ears and say "*Lalalalala!*"

Anyway, I, underfed or not, look much more like a Danish prince than Fuli does.

Still, as I waited to audition, my heart felt jumpy and my throat felt tight, and I tried to figure out why, and I decided it was fear of my own stupid body. What if I was standing there onstage and it rebelled and I went mute or belched or fainted or farted right in the middle of "To be, or not to be?"

Other people must've been nervous too, because instead of talking, they had their scripts open, and they were reading silently or mumble-mouthing the words. For a bunch of sixth graders, so much quiet was unnatural.

Meanwhile, Coach Fig was perched on the edge of the stage, headset in place, talking to someone in the great faraway. "White canvas? What about grass stains?"

Clive and I were sitting in row C, a row behind everybody else. Clive's legs are so long, he pretty much has to be on the aisle. He elbowed me. "Noah." He sounded serious, which was weird.

"What?"

"Let's make a pact. There's not enough boys, right? So we're both gonna get parts."

I nodded.

"But maybe not good parts."

"Speak for yourself," I said, more because it was the kind of thing I always say than because I meant it.

"But no matter what," Clive went on, "we're both gonna do this. Even if we're sentries and all we get to say is 'What ho!' and wave a sword, we'll do it together."

"Is this one of your sister's ideas?" I asked.

"Kind of," he admitted. "Gillian is smart sometimes, and she was a Sixth-Grade Player."

"Sure. Okay. It's a deal," I said, and we clasped hands. "Good part, bad part, big part, little part—Clive and Noah are players together."

By this time Fig had shaken off the faraway look, risen to his feet, begun to pace the way he did on the sidelines at a game. "All right, team, let's get these tryouts going!" he hollered, turning to face us. "Are you with me, team?"

Diego said, "Heck yeah!"

Mia said, "We're behind schedule."

Brianna said, "I think I'm going to throw up."

"Now, here's the dealio," Coach Fig continued. "Five-minute time slots. Read whatever bit suits you from the show." He looked around, pointed at Clive. "Mr. Desmond? How ya doin', buddy? Missed you at baseball tryouts. You're up first. Everybody else, head out to the lobby for now and—"

A loud noise interrupted—*bang*! Had a door slammed? And then came—*whoosh*—a shivery, cold gust of air.

Before we had time to react, someone behind us cleared his throat. "Coach? Had you planned to introduce me?"

The stage lights were up, and Fig squinted into the darkness at the back of the house. "There y'are, Mike."

All of us looked around.

"Team," Fig went on, "this is Mike. He'll be helpin' us out, running these auditions on my behalf, in fact. He's got the theatrical experience I lack and time on his hands. We are lucky to have him.

"Mike? Meet the Plattsfield-Winklebottom Memorial Sixth-Grade Players."

Mike stood up. Except for the coat and the hat, he seemed to be wearing the same clothes as when I'd seen him Monday. "The pleasure is mine," he said. "And now let's get to it. 'That we would do, we should do when we would.'"

I didn't know for sure whether that was a line from

the play or not until Madeline spoke up: "Act four."

So Fig's assistant *was* the mysterious Mike after all.
Maybe Mrs. Winklebottom had helped with the permis-
sions. I hadn't told anybody but my parents about seeing Mike then not seeing him. Now I wondered, since
he was going to be around awhile, if anything else weird
would happen. Out in the lobby, the serious kids, Fuli,
Madeline, and Emma, were studying their scripts while
most people were making guesses about who Mike was.

Somebody's grandpa?

Somebody who just moved here?

"I don't care who he is, as long as he knows more
about theater than Fig," Mia said.

"He does," Madeline said, and everybody wanted
to know what she was talking about, but she looked
down at her script and wouldn't answer.

The door from the house opened, and it was
Clive, who locked eyes with me and frowned. Uh-oh.

"Not good?" I said.

He shrugged, his face more puzzled than worried. "I did all right, I guess, but that Mike guy seems
to have a different script."

"Noah, my man!" Fig appeared in the doorway.
"You're up, buddy. Let's see what ya got."

CHAPTER EIGHT

I have wanted to be an actor ever since I figured out the people in TV and movies were not just living their real lives on camera; they were doing a job, and the job was to act out stories.

If I were somebody else's kid, by now I would've been to drama camp in the summer and I would have tried out for local theaters around Plattsfield, and—maybe—I would have gone to New York City and auditioned for Broadway and gotten a big part and won awards and moved to Hollywood and met big stars . . . and . . . and . . .

But, like he's always saying, my dad thinks theater is okay for entertainment, not for falling in love with, only a phase. So I don't bring it up much at Family Dinners or at any other time, either. I believe it was Polonius who said "Beware of entrance to a quarrel."

Which is why my drama experience equals watching YouTube and movies and musicals at the college, listening to *Hamilton* and *Hadestown* on repeat, and (of course) faithfully attending the annual Plattsfield-Winklebottom Memorial Sixth-Grade Play.

That's a long way of saying I don't know anything about acting except it seems to me you have to put some oomph into it, stand out, go boffo or go home.

I got laughs for my recitation, right?

So for my audition, I tried the same schtick as before—the somersault—but this time I spun around quick to face the house, waggled my thumbs at my face, and said: "'This is I, Hamlet the Dane!'" which is a line I happen to remember from act five.

Mike was sitting in the middle of the house, and Fig was pacing and gesturing in the glow of an exit sign in the back.

Mike nodded. "Unusual interpretation. And what will you be reading for me, Noah?"

"'To be or not to be,'" I said. "The famous soliloquy."

Mike nodded. "Carry on."

"Do you need to find the page?" I asked.

"Not necessary. Whenever you're ready."

I stood up straight, put my right hand on my heart, raised my chin, and let 'er rip:

"'To be or not to be . . .

"'What kind of question is that? Rather, I say, do be, do be, do . . .

"'And yet: Eschew the nap!

"'For what doth napping yield but arrows, bad luck, and nightmares?

"''Tis true, 'tis pity, 'tis pity 'tis true that life can be a bummer and dreams reveal no more the undiscovered country—'"

"Stop, Noah! PLEASE! It's painful!"

Looking back, I think Mike had been trying to interrupt for a while, but I had been very busy acting. "Did I do something wrong?"

Mike was on his feet. "Where on God's green earth did you get that drivel?"

Drivel? It was Shakespeare! I pointed to my script.

Mike looked ready to hyperventilate. "I thought perhaps Mr. Desmond was improvising, but now . . ." He flipped through the pages, then stared. "Who would dare to bowdlerize the Bard?"

"Bowdlerize the Bard"—ha! My dad had used the exact same words.

Meanwhile, Fig was striding down the aisle. "Now, now, Coach Mike. Let's all just take a mo to chillax, whaddaya say?"

"Something"—Mike held the script between thumb and forefinger—"is rotten at Plattsfield-Winklebottom!"

"The script, you mean?" Fig shook his head. "It came direct from Mrs. Winklebottom."

"I don't care if it came from Moses!" Mike said. "It's an abomination!"

Mike went on that way for a while, spewing air like an undone balloon.

When finally he stopped to breathe, Fig was ready. "Feel better? Now let me explain. Opening night is May 8. I may not know much about this play business, but I know about season openers. If you're gonna be ready, if you're gonna be a team, if you're gonna show 'em what you're made of, you gotta practice, and that means sticking to the schedule. If you can't see your way clear to help, Mike, that's your lookout—no harm, no foul. Just let me know now so we can move on. Have I made myself clear?"

Mike's arms were crossed over his chest, and his eyes were on his shoes. He mumbled something.

"What was that?" Fig asked.

Mike looked up. "You're absolutely right, Coach. Sorry for being a prima donna. I made a commitment. I'll stick to it."

"Good man," Fig said. Then he cocked his head, glanced down at his phone, raised a finger. "So sorry, guys. Gotta take this. Champagne Catering? Thanks for calling back. . . ."

Mike's shoulders slumped, and he sighed. For a second I thought he'd forgotten I was there.

"Uh, Mike?" I said. "So I can keep going?"

Mike looked up. "Yes, Noah. Continue."

I shook myself back into character—*I'm a prince, a prince, a gosh-darned prince!*—and read the remaining lines, which concluded:

"'Tis true, 'tis clear, and we can all agree,

"'Long-lived and healthy is the way to be.'"

"Oh, dear heaven," Mike murmured. "Thank you, Noah. Please send in the next actor."

"Sure. Uh, so when do we find out who got which part?" I asked.

Mike was writing on a clipboard. "I'll post the cast list tomorrow. That will give you time to take a look at your parts before the first read-through."

But how did I do? I wanted to ask. *Do you want me to try it again—without an interruption?*

But I didn't ask those questions. They seemed uncool. Maybe the next day everything would be clear.

CHAPTER NINE

Thursday, Rehearsal Week One, 43 Days till Performance

The next day one thing was clear: I didn't get cast as Hamlet.

Instead, I was cast as Marcellus, Gravedigger One, Rosencrantz, and Fortinbras, four unimportant characters no one even remembers.

One lucky thing: The only audience to witness my humiliation in real time was Clive. He and I had run to the auditorium to see the list posted on the door before anybody else.

"Awww, *man*," Clive said. "I am sorry. I thought for sure—"

"Shut up," I said.

"Excuse me?" Clive said.

"Sorry," I said, and wiped something out of my eye.

Clive must've thought it was a tear, which it cer-

tainly was not, because he frowned and got all sympathetic. "Awww, *man.*"

"It's *fine,*" I said.

"You can't quit, man," Clive said. "We made a
pact."

"I'm gonna quit anyway," I said.

"Aw, come on, man. That's not like you. I guess
it's pretty humiliating, though, huh?"

"Way to be my best friend, Clive."

"Merely speaking truth."

More people were coming up by this time, including Fuli—who had gotten the part of Hamlet instead
of me.

Fuli!

Seriously?

How was she supposed to convince an audience
she was a Danish prince?

Like they were happening all at once, I felt the sting
of the worst embarrassments of my life—the time I was
three and couldn't hold it anymore and peed my pants
in the toothpaste aisle at Duane Reade, the time I tried
to dive into the lake and belly flopped instead and had
the wind knocked out of me and had to be rescued
from drowning by Gillian, the time I barfed on the bus
coming back from the field trip to Lake Placid.

Looked at one way, the life of Noah McNichol was an extended red-faced, cringe-making humiliation.

Meanwhile, everybody else had gathered, and most people were laughing, jostling, high-fiving—even Lila and Eddie and Brianna, whose parts were as puny as mine.

The exception was Mia Duffy.

"Excuse me!" she said. "Excuse me? Stage manager? I don't want to be stage manager! I *want* to be Ophelia!"

"I wanted to be Ophelia, too," Emma said. "But *I* would never whine about it. My mother says whining is *always* unattractive."

Madeline had been cast as Ophelia. She said, "My mom used to be a manager at Denny's."

Marley said, "Don't be sad, Mia. It makes a lot of sense. My brother was stage manager. He says you get to boss everyone around."

Mia looked surprised. "Really?"

Marley nodded. "You tell the cast where to be when. You say raise the curtain and lower it. You tell the tech crew when to bring up the lights. No stage manager, no show."

The frown line between Mia's eyebrows deepened, which might've meant she was thinking.

Meanwhile, Clive was smiling, which I first thought was disloyal. Hey! I, his best friend, had suffered colossal, humiliating, horrible disappointment!

Then I realized that he, *my* best friend, had just gotten exactly the part he wanted: Claudius, the villain. And I hadn't even said props.

So who was disloyal?

And who was threatening to go back on a deal?

Some things are worse than failing to get what you want. Like being a jerk to your best friend. Like being uncool.

If I quit, everybody would know I was upset, crushed, devastated, a weakling . . . a wuss.

Truth? I was all those things and angry, too. What did this Mike guy know? Where did he even come from? If Miss Magnus were here, she would have cast me, and I'd be playing Hamlet, and the solar system and the galaxy and all the stars would be in order.

I wanted to kick something, punch something, scream at the sky.

Put my full jerkhood on display, in other words.

I could do that.

Or . . . I could do some acting for real.

I took a breath. I gulped. I wasn't going to forget this humiliation. I wasn't going to forget that I was angry. But I was a Plattsfield-Winklebottom Memorial Sixth-Grade Player. I wasn't going to quit, either.

"Hey, Fuli, congratulations," I said. "You must've read really well because, uh . . . *I* read really well."

Fuli had been staring at the cast list. Now she turned, looked straight at me, and raised one eyebrow, like she couldn't decide if I meant what I was saying.

Which made sense. I couldn't decide if I meant what I was saying.

Finally, I must've passed the sincerity test. "Thank you, Noah. I guess I did." Then she smiled, which made her look even less like a melancholy Dane than usual. It also made it hard to be mad at her.

"Hey, man." I punched Clive's arm. "Good going. I mean it. I guess I don't have to be Hamlet."

Taped to the auditorium door, the full cast and crew list looked like this:

Hamlet—Fuli Tenzing
Claudius—Clive Desmond
Gertrude—Sarah Monti
Polonius—Emma Jessel
Horatio—Diego Arcati
Ophelia—Madeline Howard
Laertes—Marley Jacobs

The Ghost, Guildenstern, Osric—Eddie Muir
Marcellus, Gravedigger One, Rosencrantz, Fortinbras—
  Noah McNichol
Cornelius, Gravedigger Two, Francisco—Brianna Larkin
Barnardo, Voltimand, Reynaldo—Lila Moseley
Stage Manager—Mia Duffy

The Plattsfield-Winklebottom Memorial Sixth-Grade Players didn't use stagehands. Cast members would be opening and closing the main curtain and moving scenery around. There was one other crew job, light and sound board operator, which meant sitting on a stool in the booth above the house, moving switches and faders. That person hadn't been picked yet. Fig would have to recruit someone.

Clive was looking at me. "So . . . you're not gonna quit?"

"I'm not gonna quit," I said. "But I do have a question. Who is Fortinbras anyway?"

Clive shrugged. "Heck if I know. He must come in at the party scene at the end."

(SCENE: Dining room, early evening the same day. NOAH, DAD, and MOM are eating dinner.)
DAD: The gravedigger's a good part, Noah. Funny.

The byplay between you and Hamlet—it's like a comedy routine.

MOM: And when you think of it, all those parts together? They probably add up to more lines than even Hamlet has.

DAD: I bet that mysterious director fellow saw you as versatile. Giving you different parts, it's a compliment really.

NOAH (*embarrassed, shaking head*): Okay, parentals. Enough with the mushy-gushy. You win at being supportive. But after I had time to think, you know what really made me feel better?

MOM and DAD (together): What?

NOAH: Since Fuli's playing the lead, there for sure will be dumplings at rehearsals.

CHAPTER TEN

Monday, Rehearsal Week Two, 39 Days till Performance

That Monday, like every Monday, Mom shook me awake, and I said, "Five more minutes," and she said, "Get up or we'll be late," and I said, "Two more minutes," never opening my eyes.

Mom went away.

But then I remembered that the first read-through was that afternoon. And even though I wasn't playing Hamlet, I was excited. So I opened my eyes and saw—like I did every morning—the poster of Obi-Wan Kenobi autographed by Alec Guinness, the actor who played him in the original movies. "Help me, Obi-Wan," I said.

And then I closed my eyes and counted to ten and rolled out of bed—Ta-da! It is I, Fortinbras!

Fortinbras, it turns out, is a Norwegian prince, so even though it's not the main prince, I still got to play a prince. And isn't Norway bigger than Denmark?

School happened. There might have been a quiz on Asian capitals. I might not have done that well.

But never mind because at 3:15 p.m., Clive and I and Fuli and Mia and Madeline and Emma and Diego and all the other Plattsfield-Winklebottom Memorial Sixth-Grade Players shoved and squealed our way into the auditorium with our scripts, ready to go, ready to read, ready to start rehearsals for real.

"'Come sit down, every mother's son, and rehearse your parts,'" Mike said, which I guess was his way to say hey, hi, come on in.

"Excuse me?" Mia said. "What about the daughters?"

"It's from another Shakespeare play, *A Midsummer Night's Dream*," Madeline said. "Act one."

"Oh," Mia said.

Onstage, fifteen folding chairs were set up in a circle. I took a spot next to Clive. Emma came up, smiled a big friendly smile, and took the chair on the other side. Emma was not known to be the friendliest person, so this was a little weird, but I didn't think that much about it.

"Where's Coach Fig?" Mia asked.

Mike looked puzzled. "Coach who?" he said. "Ah."

He got it. "Coach Newton is meeting with the mother of the bride, I believe. He will check in later. As for us, there is no time to waste. Go ahead and get out your scripts, please. Miss Duffy? Most productions relegate the stage manager to the tech booth, but given the size of our operation, I'm going to ask you to stay backstage the night of the performance. Meanwhile, I have some things for you—the two items without which no stage manager can do her job: a clipboard for taking notes and a stopwatch for keeping time."

He presented them, and Mia grinned, delighted.

"As stage manager," Mike continued, "you will be expected to set the scene prior to each rehearsal—the place and time, in other words. Start the stopwatch running first, and then please proceed."

Mia touched the watch to start it, then sat up straight. "The scene is Elsinore, a castle in Denmark. The time is shortly after midnight."

"Just so," Mike said. "Miss Moseley—Lila? You are playing Barnardo, a guard on overnight duty at the castle. He and his fellow sentry, Marcellus, believe they have seen a ghost the previous couple of nights. Now Barnardo is wondering if the ghost will appear again."

"Oka-a-ay, so, like, you want me to start now?" Lila said.

"Whenever you're ready," Mike said.

Lila bobbed her head. "Oka-a-ay. So, like, here I go. 'Sit down awhile, and let us once again assail your ears, that are so fortified against our story, what we have two nights seen.'"

Diego, playing Horatio, had the next line. But instead of speaking, he tugged the hat he was wearing, adjusted his round glasses, and stared down at his script.

"Mr. Arcati—Diego?" Mike said. "You're up."

"I know, but . . ."

"The language is not what you're used to," Mike said, "but in time you'll get the hang of it. 'Sit we down, and let us hear Barnardo speak of this.' Go ahead. Dig in and *inhabit* the character. You are Horatio, Hamlet's best friend, a young man very eager to know the truth about the ghost."

Diego didn't look convinced but nodded and read Horatio's line. Then Barnardo spoke, then me as Marcellus: "'Peace! Break thee off! Look, where it comes again.'"

Inhabit the character, I thought, and I tried to sound like a guy who'd just seen a ghost—surprised I mean, which wasn't that hard because I really was surprised: Something weird was going on.

Leave it to Mia to comment first.

"Excuse me!" she said.

Mike looked up. "Yes? Miss Duffy?"

Mia brandished her script. "I read this over the weekend. I made notes even. And now the words are different."

Marley said, "Also the print got smaller."

Sarah said, "Also there are more pages."

Brianna said, "This is totally freaking me out."

"May I?" Mike took Mia's script, squinted at it, flipped through the pages, looked at Mia. "Are these your notations in the margins? Purple ink?"

"That's my handwriting, but . . ." Mia's voice trailed off.

Mike handed back the script. "Then I think we can all agree it must be your script."

"Heck yeah!" Diego said.

Everybody looked at Diego, whose hat—the beret kind from France, a little like a Frisbee if you ask me—was turquoise that day. He must have a whole collection of those hats.

"Did you even read the play?" Mia asked Diego.

"Quite a bit of it. A page at least," Diego said.

I didn't know what was going on, either, but it felt awkward. Like someone was making a joke, and maybe the joke was on us.

Then Madeline said, "'There are more things in heaven and earth, Horatio, than are dreamt of in your philosophy.'"

Mike looked pleased. "Act one, and very appropriate, Miss Howard. Hamlet is speaking to his friend after he's met the ghost. What do you suppose he means? Anyone?"

"That the world is complicated?" Fuli tried.

"Indeed," Mike said. "And remember that Horatio is a student. So Hamlet is saying the world is larger, contains more mysteries, than those you learn about in school. Now"—Mike looked around at each of us—"what if we choose to view this vastly improved script as that kind of a mystery, something beyond mere human understanding?"

Mia frowned. "So should I pause the stopwatch or what?"

Emma said, "My mother says there's a *reasonable* explanation for *everything*."

Marley said, "Depends on your definition of reason, I guess."

Brianna said, "I'm still freaking out."

"All good responses," Mike said, "and all, at present, pale before one imperative: The show must go on! And for that to happen, we must stick to the schedule. I'm sure, Miss Duffy, you agree?"

Mia looked down at her watch. "We're way behind already."

"Miss Moseley?" Mike said, "I believe the next line is yours."

The read-through continued. We only had ninety minutes. The way they talked in Shakespeare's time isn't the way we talk now. We had to stop a lot for translation. Still, we made it through the parts where Hamlet stabs Polonius to death by accident and, after that, Ophelia is so sad she goes crazy and drowns herself.

I didn't know what had happened to our scripts, whether Mike had pulled some kind of trick or what, but by the end of the read-through, I didn't care that much. This *Hamlet* was way better than the other one! Just like Madeline had promised, it was intense! And I couldn't wait to see what happened in the end.

CHAPTER ELEVEN

Dad had a department meeting that afternoon. Since I knew he'd be late picking me up, I stayed and helped Mike fold chairs and put them away backstage.

Here was my chance to ask why he hadn't cast me as Hamlet, and I was ready, but before I could open my mouth, he said, "How do you think that went, Noah? I don't have much experience with your age group. The kids seemed attentive enough, wouldn't you say?"

"Sure," I said, because what else would I say? "That was weird about the scripts, though."

"But I handled it all right?"

"Sure. Only I'm not sure Mrs. Winklebottom would like the new script very much. I can imagine her saying, 'Inappropriate for children!'"

"And is it inappropriate? What do you think?" Mike stood in the middle of the stage, holding the last chair.

I had one last chair, too. I set it down. "I've seen scarier things. But the words are hard. A lot of them I don't know. Maybe Emma or somebody smart does, but not me."

Mike grinned. "Are you up to the challenge?"

So far I had the idea that Mike was a serious person. But when he grinned, you had to grin back. "Sure. Yes. Only—" And then I was going to ask him about not casting me, but a door opened backstage, I heard footsteps, and Coach Fig came in through the wings.

"Sorry I'm just getting here. How did it go?" he asked. "Darned venue."

What's a venue? I wondered.

"Location for an event such as a wedding," Mike said. "A hotel or a country club, for example."

I nodded, and . . . wait a sec. I hadn't asked that question out loud, had I?

"Let me get those," Fig said. He took the last two chairs, carried them backstage, came back.

"Planning a wedding must be quite a challenge," Mike said.

"The planning's okay. It's the people that make ya nuts," Fig said.

Mike spoke another line from the play. "'What a piece of work is a man, how noble in reason, how infinite in faculty . . . and yet man delights me not.'"

Fig nodded. "Got that right. And women are no picnic, either. Look, if you're okay here, I got a few more calls to make. I'll come back around to lock up."

"Of course. We'll see you next time." Mike saluted the departing coach, then slid the green-glowing iPad thing from his coat pocket, swiped at the screen, stared at it. "I have another question for you, Noah. The schedule says something about a parent meeting next week."

"A lot of the parents volunteer," I said, "like, to make costumes or work on the set. So I guess it's to organize all that."

Mike frowned. "Hmmm. Organizing parents is not what I signed up for. And besides, I have my own, uh . . . methods for realizing the set and the costumes. Do you think the parents will mind if we cancel? Or possibly Coach Newton can channel their efforts in another direction."

I shrugged. "Mine won't mind. They're pretty busy. Can I ask you something?"

"Of course, Noah."

"Why didn't you cast me as Hamlet?" There. I had said it.

Mike took a breath. "Yes, well. I thought we might come around to that. Your audition showed . . ." He didn't finish the sentence. Instead, he looked up. "'Methinks I scent the morning air.'"

"Act one," I said automatically, "right? But my audition . . . ?"

Only I didn't find out about my audition.

Because the next instant Mike vanished.

This time wasn't like when he was on the bench and I looked away and looked back and he was gone. This time I was looking right at him . . . and then I was looking at nothing.

From behind me in the auditorium a door creaked open and my dad said, "Noah? Time to go, buddy. Who were you talking to?"

CHAPTER TWELVE

(*SCENE: Dining room, early evening the same day. NOAH, DAD, and MOM are eating dinner.*)

DAD: Noah? Earth to Noah. Would you like more soup?

NOAH (*blinks*): Wh-what? Soup?

MOM: Honey, you've been acting strange ever since you got home from school.

DAD: And you were white as a ghost when I picked you up.

NOAH (*widens eyes*) White as . . . ?

MOM (*leans over, puts palm on NOAH's forehead, speaks to DAD*): He doesn't have a fever.

NOAH (*shakes hand away*): I'm fine. Sorry. Thinking is all.

DAD: Would you care to enlighten us as to what you're thinking about?

NOAH: Uh . . . the play? *Hamlet.* It's really violent.

MOM: Is it? I thought you were doing that No-Trauma nonsense Mrs. Winklebottom favors. Happily ever after, the end.

NOAH: We were, but . . . (*stares for a second, blinks, focuses*) but now our scripts have Shakespeare's own words, and the plot's different, too.

MOM: Oh good. I don't like dumbed-down versions for kids.

DAD: Where did that No-Trauma business come from in the first place? I wonder.

MOM (*wags thumbs at herself*): I know. *I* heard all about it at Sal's.

DAD: So tell.

MOM: Once upon a time—

NOAH: *Mom.*

MOM: It's a story! Once upon a time, a very long time ago, Mrs. Winklebottom was a sixth-grade teacher herself, only then she was Miss something-or-other, and she organized and directed the first Sixth-Grade Play, which was *Richard III*—

DAD: Shakespeare wrote that one too.

MOM: —about a killer king, and if anything, it's even bloodier than *Hamlet.* So the performance happens, and everyone's in awe of the kids for handling the language and poetry and so forth and Miss Whatever is basking in glory until the next day when—instead of roses and a hearty thank-you—she gets a note from John Winklebottom—

DAD: The plot thickens!

MOM: —who's the chairman of the school board, and he tells her sixth graders are too young for blood and evil, she's corrupting them, and what if they got the idea it's okay to question authority, like for example kings and school board chairpersons and teachers and principals? And, oh, by the way, if she wants to keep teaching, she better not put on any more plays like *Richard III*. (*She takes a breath, spoons up soup.*)

DAD: He threatened her?

MOM: Basically. And I guess she needed the job because she came around to his point of view about delicate sixth graders, and not only that—

NOAH: Wait a sec. His name was Winklebottom? And hers wasn't Winklebottom at the time, so does that mean—

MOM (*nods*): Somehow or another, Mr. Winklebottom, who was not only the chairman of the school board, but he also owned the sawmill down by the lake, convinced her to use No-Trauma Drama scripts in the future, and eventually he also convinced her to marry him.

DAD: Maybe she convinced him.

MOM *(shrugs)*: Maybe she did.

NOAH: I never knew Mrs. Winklebottom used to be a teacher. And I never heard of any Mr. Winklebottom.

MOM: Like I said, a long time ago. After she got married, she quit teaching. Eventually, Mr. Winklebottom died, and they renamed the school, and she got the sawmill and the money, some of which she donated for the Sixth-Grade Play, which was stuck with No-Trauma Drama forevermore.

NOAH *(staunchly)*: I'm in sixth grade, and I'm old enough for blood and evil.

DAD: Is that a good thing?

MOM: Dumbed-down literature confuses kids. They get to my classes at the college and think they know the stories, but they don't.

DAD: Anyway, it's a tempest in a teapot.

NOAH: Teapot . . . what?

MOM: It means make a big deal out of something that's trivial. (*She looks at DAD.*) And I'd like to know what you mean by *that*, dear. Shakespeare's trivial? Kids are trivial?

DAD: Now, don't get all riled—

MOM: I teach English!

DAD: I realize that. But you have to admit that in the end, knowing Shakespeare doesn't count for much in today's world. Science, math, engineering— those are the disciplines we need to tackle the climate emergency, clean up the planet, make a world that future generations can inhabit.

MOM *(staring incredulously at DAD)*: And I wonder what we have that's worth saving if not culture, which includes the arts, which includes theater, which includes Shakespeare the way he wrote it, not the way Mrs. Winklebottom wants it to be.

NOAH *(looking from one to the other, anxious)*: Are you guys gonna get divorced?

MOM: Maybe.

DAD: No.

MOM: Apologies, Noah. I did not mean that. We are not getting divorced.

NOAH: Other people's parents get divorced. Like Eddie Muir's. Like Dad's.

DAD: Reasonable people can disagree without getting divorced.

MOM: Or, in your dad's case, unreasonable people.

· · ·

So my dad and mom were mad at each other, which wasn't great, but when I went to bed it wasn't No. 1 on my mind, either.

No. 1 on my mind was freaking out because right around four hours earlier, Mike, our new director, had *disappeared in front of my very eyes!*

I had put off freaking out because my parents would've worried if they thought I'd gone bonkers (like Ophelia). So I had acted normal right through dinner and homework and a couple of games of *Shred-Sauce* (Clive crushed me; I may have been distracted), after which I said good night, brushed my teeth, put on pajamas, closed my door, turned out the light, and threw myself facedown on the pillow.

How had Mike done it? Why had he done it? What possibility made disappearing possible?

I thought of *Star Trek* and time travel and mirrors in magic shows. I thought of Harry Potter and the other wizards who could apparate. I wondered if there was something wrong with my eyes. I remembered something called mass hypnosis and wondered if Mike had ever even been in Plattsfield at all, if someone had hypnotized us to believe he had.

I even thought, so, okay, Mike disappeared, but shouldn't his clothes have stuck around?

In the famous soliloquy, Hamlet says the trouble with dying is that it might be like sleeping and you might have nightmares. That night, though, sleep came to my rescue, and if I had bad dreams, I forgot them.

Mom woke me as usual; as usual I put off getting up. But by that time my brain had stopped spinning; I knew I wasn't crazy.

My eyes are fine. Except for Clive, I am the most normal kid I know. And therefore Mike really did disappear. And the script swap? And answering a question I had asked only in my head?

Maybe those were clues to a mystery.

And mysteries I know about. When I was a kid—not that long ago—I read every single detective story starring Nate the Great.

So I made a decision. I wouldn't tell anybody what I'd seen . . . not seen . . . stopped seeing. Not until I understood it. Bad enough I didn't get cast as Hamlet. I didn't need to get teased, another humiliation. Plus, I didn't actually want to make trouble for Mike, because what if I did and Fig had to direct the play? What if we had to go back to the old, boring script?

That would be disaster! (As Brianna would say.)

Whatever happened, the show must go on.

I took a breath, opened my eyes, spoke to my *Star Wars* poster: "Help me, Obi-Wan." Then I rolled out of bed, ready to face another day of sixth grade.

CHAPTER THIRTEEN

Tuesday, Rehearsal Week Two, 38 Days till Performance

At lunch, most of us drama geeks sit at the same table. I mean, not Fuli because she never sits with us, and not Diego because nobody knows where he goes at lunch, and not Eddie Muir because he sits with the jocks.

But everyone else.

The caf serves meals in a two-week rotation, and that day was lasagna, which is actually one of the caf's better recipes even though the orange sauce, which turns your tongue and teeth orange too, is probably radioactive, according to Clive who heard it from Gillian.

Everybody wanted to talk about the mysterious script swap, of course, but it turned out there wasn't that much to say except "That sure was mysterious," so then the conversation shifted to *Hamlet,* the play itself.

Brianna said, "I don't understand even one single word, and I'll never learn the lines, and we're all going to look like fools in front of our families and everyone in the whole town and my relatives from Poughkeepsie."

Emma said, "*My* parents say that *my* character, Polonius, is the very wisest one."

Madeline said, "No, Emma, he's not. Shakespeare calls him a 'foolish prating knave.'"

Brianna said, "That's exactly what I'm worried about! What even *is* 'prating'?"

"And like, 'knave,' too, right?" Lila asked.

Before anyone could answer, Emma told Madeline she'd better take that back about Polonius, and Madeline said, "Who better take what back?" and Mia said, "On the other hand, if the shoe fits," and Emma wanted to know why *everybody* was ganging up on her, and Marley said nobody was ganging up on her, and Clive shook his head and said, "Another episode of *Lunchtime Drama.*"

"Brought to you by today's cafeteria special: radioactive lasagna," I added.

"The only lasagna that glows in the dark," said Clive.

And everybody laughed, and nobody got up and

79

stomped away leaving half their lunch behind, or burst into tears, like happens sometimes—especially, TBH, the girls.

What is with girls anyway?

Mostly I don't know or care. I am happy to be a skinny dude with slightly stick-out ears and freckles and red*dish* hair, a dude girls don't care about—a dude who doesn't care about them, either, I mean—except the way I care about and respect all my fellow humans, of course, even if I don't go to church or temple.

Then again, sometimes I get curious about who's in and who's out and how come, and when I do, I ask Clive.

Clive notices stuff, like say if Marley and Brianna—who are usually best friends—aren't speaking, or say Emma and Mia, who most of the time hate each other, have formed an alliance against Sarah, who is the prettiest girl in the class and wears a bra and sometimes even makeup.

Why does Clive notice? Because, courtesy of Gillian, he's seen all six seasons of *Gossip Girl.*

After we got distracted from Polonius, the conversation shifted to, "Do you like Mike?"

"Yeah, sure," I said. "I mean, even though he made

the tragic choice to cast Fuli instead of me as Hamlet, he seems like a good guy. And he knows a lot."

"I don't like him," Emma said, which did not actually surprise me.

"Oh no, Emma—do you think he's an *escaped convict?*" Brianna asked.

Emma narrowed her eyes. "Maybe. *Probably. My* parents think *someone* should look into his background."

"Sounds like a job for D. Avventura," Marley said.

Everybody laughed . . . except me. I said, "Who?"

"That guy on PicPoc. Come on, Noah, even *you* must've seen the PW PicPoc," Mia said.

I had a choice here: A) admit to being ignorant, or B) pretend I knew something I didn't know. Reasoning that ignorance was what everybody expected from me anyway, I chose A. "Nope."

"Oh, my man." Clive looked at me and shook his head sorrowfully.

Maybe I should've gone with B?

"*I'll* explain," said Emma, and she gave me that bright smile again, which I guess was better than rolling her eyes, but at the same time kind of weirded me out. "PW is Plattsfield-Winklebottom, of course, and PicPoc is that app where you make short movies?

81

Except you're not supposed to be on it unless you're at least thirteen, so whoever D. Avventura really is, I think he must be breaking the rules!"

"Uh-huh," I said, worried everyone was looking at me.

"And this D. Avventura person has been making a whole bunch of these short movie things about our school, and calling them PW PicPocs, only no one knows who he is, or she is, or they are, I mean, for that matter."

"And they're funny," Marley said. "The PW PicPocs, that is."

"They're kind of *mean*," Brianna said. "Some of them."

"But like everybody watches them?" Lila said. "Because you kind of can't wait to see what D. Avventura will do next? You know?"

"But I don't get it," I said. "What are they about?"

"Many subjects," Mia said. "There was one about chess, only the king had Mr. Long's face—you know, the principal? And there was one about lacrosse where the whole team got pummeled with sticks. What else?"

"The one about the canoe was cool," Sarah said. "The boat flipped and all you could see was bubbles."

"So *scary!*" said Brianna.

The bell rang. We gathered up our trays and back-packs and jackets. To get to the main classroom building from the caf, you have to go outside. About half the people actually put their jackets on and zipped them up. The rest of us clutched our jackets and got ready to dash.

Next to me by the door, Madeline tugged my sleeve. "Don't feel bad, Noah. I never heard of PW PicPocs either."

CHAPTER FOURTEEN

There was no rehearsal that day, and after school, I asked myself a question: What would Nate the Great do?

I was home. Clive's mom had dropped me off. My own mom's last class was at two, and she wouldn't be home till around four thirty, so just a normal Tuesday except for my personally assigned homework, which was to solve the case of the mysterious disappearing director.

I grabbed a box of Cheez-Its, a glass of milk, and an apple, went downstairs to the family room/basement where my family's hulking dinosaur of a computer sleeps on a hulking dinosaur of a desk.

When Nate the Great solves a mystery, he buttons up his raincoat, pulls down his Sherlock Holmes–style hat, and pounds the pavement in search of clues. He also eats a lot of pancakes.

I didn't have the coat or the hat or the pancakes.

But I did have something Nate didn't: the Internet.

I sat myself on the desk chair, swiveled one fast rotation for luck, tapped the power key. A few seconds passed, like the machine had to yawn and stretch to wake up. During those seconds I thought about the most logical way to search, the best question to ask. Then I typed, "What does it mean if the person you're talking to disappears?"

People disappearing can't be that usual, but I got a zillion results. The first three were ads—romance advice, a paranormal investigator, a horror movie on Netflix. After that came the Wikipedia entry on "paranormal phenomena," which I clicked on and learned that in Jamaica they call ghosts duppies.

Interesting but not helpful.

Usually the second page of search results is useless, but I went there anyway, and at the top was this: **How to Tell if the Entity You're Talking to Is a Ghost.**

Somewhere, Nate the Great smiled.

The website was normal-looking except for a picture up in the corner, a logo I guess, of a cartoon ghost wearing an old-fashioned businessman's hat, the same kind Mike wears. One other thing: The background—the wallpaper, they call it—was the same brown plaid pattern as Mike's coat.

Weird coincidence, huh?

I read fast through the words—"grateful acknowledgment . . . Society of Ghostly Investigations . . . public service . . . spirit of health or goblin damned . . ."

I stopped and read the last part over. The idea was the site would help you decide if you were facing a good ghost or a bad ghost, but I knew that goblin line. *Hamlet, Act I.*

I thought of that movie, whatzitcalled that starts with a *P*, where the TV sucks in the little girl. Should I unplug the computer and run?

Nate the Great is not known for extreme bravery. Still, I couldn't remember a time he actually ran away. Without pancakes, I took a fierce bite of apple, chewed hard, and went to the next screen, which showed the first question in one of those online quiz things: **Did the entity in question disappear while you were talking to him, her, or it?**

The options were to click yes or no, so of course I clicked yes.

Second question: Was the entity that disappeared wearing clothing long out of style?

Yes.

Were you looking directly at the entity when it disappeared?

Yes.

Did you experience associated evidence of supernatural phenomena?

I had to translate that one. In the end, I decided it meant, Did anything else weird happen? I clicked yes.

Please check all that apply:

❏ Unexplained cold drafts of air

❏ Spoken answer to a question never asked out loud

❏ Replacement of the unpardonably inferior by the surpassingly superior, e.g. bowdlerized Shakespeare by real Shakespeare

❏ Ridiculously pertinent Internet search results

❏ Clanking chains, otherwise invisible faces reflected in mirror, predawn howling, animation of ordinarily inanimate objects (e.g., vases, tables, chairs).

These questions stopped me cold. Like literally. I felt a chill.

Help me, Nate the Great!

I tried to stay logical. Clive was about one thousand

times better with technology than me. Had he done something to my computer? But he didn't even know I was down here trying to solve the mystery. Maybe kids from the college?

But why would they care enough about this computer, or about me, to go to the trouble?

I didn't know what was going on, and I was a little scared, but I was also annoyed. Someone was messing with me. Fine. I would mess with them back. So I checked the first four, which were all true, and then I checked the fifth one, which wasn't.

Click the left arrow to return to previous screen and tell the truth. Or, to continue, click continue.

Oh yeah? Be that way. I clicked continue.

Look, do you want to know if he's a ghost or not?

Now the Cheez-Its in my gut threatened rebellion. I swallowed hard, took a deep breath, made myself calm down, clicked yes.

Congratulations! You are dealing with a bona fide spirit of health, aka a ghost, and not a goblin damned. Please treat him or her with the utmost deference, and don't forget to have your lines memorized by Monday, April 13, when you go off-book.

Wait—did I even read that?

I couldn't go back and check.

I barely had time to react because *Pop!* went the speakers and *Fizz!* came a hail of sparks, which filled the screen in rainbow colors before fading slowly to black. At last a single line of text appeared: We're sorry, but the website you're seeking is temporarily unavailable. Please try again later or, alternatively, forget all about it and move on with your life.

CHAPTER FIFTEEN

(SCENE: Split stage, Noah's bedroom on the left, Clive's on the right, taking up a bit more than half the stage. Clive's is more upscale than Noah's, very Pottery Barn. Noah's furniture seems to have been handed down after lots of love from the previous generation. In common: ski and snowboard posters on the walls. Noah lies against pillows on his bed with his phone to his ear. Clive, equipped with Bluetooth earbuds, sits in a recliner looking at a tablet.)

NOAH: You're gonna think I'm crazy.

CLIVE *(playing a game as he talks, distracted)*: Uh-huh, and that would be different from every day exactly how?

NOAH: Clive! I need you to stop playing *Candy Crush* and pay attention!

CLIVE *(blinks, sits up)*: *Candy Crush?* I would never—

NOAH: Mike is a ghost! Don't ask me how I know.

(*CLIVE reacts slowly—shakes head, widens eyes, straightens back, scratches head, looks out window as if to say: Wha'?*)

NOAH: Hello? Are you still there? What are you doing?

CLIVE (*rises from chair, paces downstage*): Playing *Candy Crush.* Oh—and wondering whether to call 911 this second or wait till morning.

NOAH: Don't make fun of me, Clive. I wouldn't've told you, but I had to tell somebody. It's like the secret was busting out of me.

CLIVE (*grins, singing*): . . . somethin' strange in the neighborhood . . . who ya gonna call?

NOAH: Not funny.

CLIVE: All right, all right. Let me get this straight. You're talking about Mike the director Mike? Old dude? Wears a funky coat?

NOAH (*exasperated*): Yes, Clive! I mean, I can't prove he's a ghost. The website went all Rice Krispies on me. But I knew something was funny, which I didn't tell you because I wanted to investigate first. So now I did and now you believe me. Don't you?

CLIVE: Nope, Noah, I don't. To borrow from the best, "These are but wild and whirling words."

NOAH: You're saying I'm crazy.

CLIVE: No offense, but it's the most reasonable conclusion.

NOAH: Clive, Mike can disappear. And read minds, I think. And he has power over the Internet, too.

CLIVE *(stops pacing, frowns, faces audience)*: Noah? Slow down a second, bro. Do you feel okay? Are your parents home?

NOAH: I can't tell my parents, Clive. They'll worry.

CLIVE: Yeah, they'll worry. I'm worried!

NOAH *(sits up angrily, collapses against pillows)*: Never mind. You're right. No ghosts. I had a brain blip.

CLIVE *(pivots, returns to recliner, sits down, still frowning)*: Good.

NOAH: One more question.

CLIVE *(suspicious)*: Yeah?

NOAH: What if I get Mike to admit to us that he's a ghost?

CHAPTER SIXTEEN

Wednesday, Rehearsal Week Two, 37 Days till Performance

In the No-Trauma Drama *Hamlet,* the last scene is a party that the Norwegian prince Fortinbras (played by me, Noah McNichol!) throws for the new king of Denmark, Hamlet.

Hamlet has become king because his uncle Claudius (Clive, the villain) realizes he messed up when he made himself king, so he takes off his crown with a flourish and gives it to Hamlet and bows.

Nobody's mad. Everybody forgives everybody else. The ghost even comes back and apologizes for being un-chill and scary.

The moral of the story is: Don't do anything big until you've taken your time and thought it over. And in case anyone in the audience has missed it, Ophelia speaks this speech:

Hamlet with a choice to make
Did dither and pontificate,
Was indecisive, noncommittal
(Just like Nero with his fiddle),
Busy with soliloquies
And really mean to his main squeeze,
But time moved forward—big surprise!
His thoughtful thinking had been wise.
In the end, he traded frown
For shiny scepter and gold crown.

After the first read-through, we Plattsfield-Winklebottom Sixth-Grade Players knew that in Shakespeare's version, Ophelia (Madeline) was too dead to be speaking verses at the end. At the second read-through, we found out almost everything else was different too.

Like, instead of a party at the end, there's a duel. And unlike Simba, Hamlet never gets to be king because Hamlet is dead, and so are Gertrude and Claudius and Laertes, and they're lying all over the stage when Fortinbras comes in and says, more or less, "What the heck happened here?"

Fortinbras, not Ophelia, speaks the last line of the real *Hamlet*: "Go, bid the soldiers shoot." He's the prince from Norway (which is way bigger than Denmark—I checked) telling his guys to fire their guns as a salute to all the royal people who died, especially Hamlet.

When I walked into the auditorium that afternoon, I stared at Mike, looking for more evidence of his ghostliness. Maybe his body would shimmer uncontrollably. Maybe his edges would blur.

None of that happened. Or, as Shakespeare would've said, his "too too solid flesh" did not melt.

As for the Plattsfield-Winklebottom Memorial Sixth-Grade Players, they were settling in as usual in a circle of folding chairs on the stage, and none of them seemed to have realized Mike was a ghost—not even Clive, not even after I told him.

In fact, I must've really freaked Clive out because all day he'd been treating me the way a parental treats a kid with the flu, asking if I felt okay. Then in the caf (chicken noodle day), he offered to carry my tray.

As soon as I took the chair next to Clive, Emma came over and sat next to me, which made no sense. She played Polonius, remember, and none of my characters even had a scene with Polonius. But *whatever.* During the read-through, the play took all my attention. In the final scene, I dug in, inhabited the character of Fortinbras, spoke that last line with feeling.

Then the auditorium went quiet. Dead quiet. The ending was so sad—bodies all over the stage—I think the Plattsfield-Winklebottom Memorial Sixth-Grade Players were in shock.

Mia was the first to recover. She checked her stopwatch. "Take five minutes, everyone. And *only* five minutes. I believe Fuli's mom came by with snacks."

"Dumplings!" said Clive. In an instant, we were all on our feet.

The dumplings were delicious, of course, and disappeared in a trice—which is how Shakespeare would have said it if he'd ever been lucky enough to eat dumplings from Fuli's family's restaurant.

Soon Mike clapped his hands. "All right, players. If you're sufficiently fortified, let's reconvene, shall we? Now, how is everybody doing? Miss Howard? Are you disappointed you won't be making that final speech?"

"It's more fun to go crazy," Madeline said.

"Good woman," Mike said.

Emma tugged her hair. "Speaking for *myself,* I'm not sure I understand what makes this *play* so great. I mean, is there even a *moral?*"

Brianna said, "Life is short, and then you die?"

I don't think Brianna meant it to be funny, but we all laughed, including Mike. "Very good, Miss Larkin. Who else thinks that's the moral?"

"Heck yeah!" said Diego.

He had his phone out, and Mike said, "Alluring as that is, Mr. Arcati, would you mind putting it away?"

"Heck no!" Diego said, but he didn't stick the phone in his pocket till after he'd snapped a quick picture.

Meanwhile, Mike had another question. "Does a story have to have a moral?"

"If it doesn't, what's the point?" Mia asked.

"Anyway, the moral's not the same as in the first script, the one from Mrs. Winklebottom," Fuli said. "It's almost like the opposite. Hamlet thinks too much, and that's why things go wrong."

We were in a circle, remember, and Fuli gestured toward the center, and we all looked and we all gasped. For an instant the crumpled bodies of Hamlet, Laertes, Gertrude, and Claudius seemed to lie before us. But then, like fog in sunshine, they disappeared, leaving us—me at least—a little shaky.

Mike said, "What fine imaginations you all have."

Everybody says imagination is good, but all those

bodies made me think Mrs. Winklebottom and the No-Trauma Drama people might've been right after all. Maybe the real *Hamlet* is too intense for sixth graders.

Mike was speaking again. I tried to pay attention. "The play is a tragedy, and tragedies happen in life as well as onstage. Consider that the artist's job is to help us make sense of that, deal with that sad fact. In act five, Horatio warns Hamlet about the duel, which is a trap set by Claudius."

Clive rubbed his hands together. "Bwaha-*ha!*" He just loved being evil.

Mike nodded. "Indeed. And what does Hamlet do, Mr. Desmond?"

"Uh . . . he decides to fight anyway," Clive said. "He says, 'I defy augury.'"

"Like, what even *is* augury?" Lila asked.

Mia said, "I looked it up. It means fate, something that's gonna happen and you can't control it."

"Let me get this straight," Brianna said. "Hamlet knows something terrible will happen if he does the duel, and then he goes and does it anyway, which means Hamlet is just plain dumb."

Mike smiled. "You're not the first to make that conclusion, Miss Larkin. But what about this? Elsewhere, Hamlet says a man is no better than a beast 'if his chief good and market of his time be but to sleep and feed.'"

"Act four," Madeline said quietly.

"I think here Shakespeare is suggesting that Hamlet is more than mere beast, that he is a hero, in fact," Mike said. "And this is not because he succeeds in defying his fate; it is because he tries."

"Kind of depressing," Marley said. "Emma's right."

Mike looked sad himself but only for a moment. When he spoke, his usual expression returned—eyebrows raised and eyeballs aimed down along his nose, aka: too cool for school. "There's something else about *Hamlet* I find interesting, a reason I think it's a particularly good play for young people."

"Does it make it less depressing?" Emma asked.

"You tell me," Mike said. "Now, consider the plot. Over and over, the older generation spies on the young. Polonius is the worst. He sends Reynaldo to spy on Polonius's own son, Laertes. Later he and Claudius spy on Hamlet and Ophelia. And later still, spying on Gertrude and Hamlet, he gets his comeuppance. He 'find'st to be too busy is some danger,' and dies."

"'Dead for a ducat, dead,'" Fuli spoke Hamlet's line.

"But Claudius does not learn the lesson," Mike went on. "*Hamlet* is a play about many things, but I believe an important one is the hopeless and nefarious way one generation tries to withhold power from the next."

Like Shakespeare himself, Mike said stuff that was fancy and hard to understand. But now I got his point, which made me think of the story Mom had told at Family Dinner, how Mr. Winklebottom worried the real version of *Richard III* would encourage kids to question authority.

William Shakespeare: revolutionary!

Emma looked alarmed. "So he's saying we shouldn't listen to our parents?"

Mike's eyes scanned our faces. "Who has parents that remind them of Gertrude, Claudius, and Polonius?"

"Mine remind me of Polonius a little," Emma said. "They like to give advice."

"Ha ha—that makes your parents 'foolish prating knaves'!" Diego said.

"Wait, like, I forget. A knave is a bad thing, right?" Lila said.

"You take that back!" Emma said.

"Lila?" Madeline said. "Or Diego?"

Mike raised a hand for quiet. "All worthy comments," he said, "but we need to move on. To summarize, the story of Hamlet is sad, but the play is beautiful. And when an artist makes beauty out of tragedy, isn't that inspiring? And isn't inspiring the opposite of depressing?"

CHAPTER SEVENTEEN

Was the play inspiring or depressing?

Not even Emma had a response to that question. Not even Mia.

Maybe they were answering in their own heads. Maybe they were thinking about rides home.

"And now"—Mike slid the glowing green iPad thing from its place in his pocket and glanced down— "on to our next meeting, which is tomorrow. We'll be blocking scenes one through five. Please get to work memorizing your parts. Long play. Short rehearsal time. As Miss Duffy would be only too happy to tell you, our schedule is all."

The Plattsfield-Winklebottom Memorial Sixth-Grade Players rose from their chairs, shuffled on backpacks and coats, clumped offstage, departed into the cold and damp.

All except me and Clive. My dad was going to be late again, but it wasn't because of a class this time. It was because I had asked him to be late.

I needed a chance to talk to Clive and Mike alone.

Folding chairs and putting them away was thirty seconds of work, and then there was an awkward moment. I looked at Mike. Clive looked at me. Mike looked back and forth between us. Finally, his eyes came to rest on my face. "Out with it, Mr. McNichol," he said. "'Screw your courage to the sticking place.'"

It's awkward, asking someone if they're a ghost.

Ever since I'd decided I was going to do it, I'd been thinking about how not to make it an insult, if it was an insult. Was "Hey, so are you a ghost?" the same as saying, "Hey, so are you super old and dead and decayed?"

And now the moment was here, and I hadn't come up with anything clever or polite.

"That courage line's not from *Hamlet*, is it?" I stalled.

"Different Shakespeare play," Mike said. "*Macbeth*. It has a ghost, too."

"Are you one? A ghost, I mean. I hope you don't mind me asking."

There. Best I could do.

For a moment, Mike continued to look down his nose at me. As for Clive—what should I call the look on his face? Exasperated? Embarrassed? Scared?

Mike answered. "Yes," then, "Boo."

I turned to Clive. His expression had frozen. "Told you," I said.

Clive swallowed hard, then mumbled, "'Words, words, words.'"

"A hit, Mr. Desmond," Mike said. "A very palpable hit."

"I'm lost," I said.

"Lines from *Hamlet*," Mike said.

"Well, I *knew* that," I said. "What I meant was—"

"Anyone can say they're a ghost, use that word," Clive said. "It doesn't prove anything."

"It doesn't," Mike agreed. "And, in fact, it doesn't matter if you believe I'm a ghost or not. What matters is that you take my direction."

Clive still seemed nervous, spooked—ha ha. But maybe a little less so. "Good deal, Mr. . . . uh?"

At that moment I realized something. Mike had never told us his last name.

"I had a full name in life," Mike said. "In death, 'Mike' is enough."

"See?" I said to Clive. "That proves he's a ghost.

He read my mind! I was wondering about his last name, and he told us."

Mike smiled. "That wasn't mind reading, Noah. That was regular human intuition. On the other hand, how about this?"

The three of us were standing center stage, Mike looking at Clive and me, his back to the wings. Now, without turning or looking over his shoulder, he said, "Emma? You can come out anytime."

And she did.

CHAPTER EIGHTEEN

Emma emerged from the darkness directly behind Mike, coated up and wearing her backpack, a confused frown on her face. "How did you—" she started to ask.

"A ghost knows." Mike turned to face her. "May I help you, Emma? Why were you eavesdropping?"

Clive gasped. "Like Polonius!"

Emma said, "*Not* like Polonius because *I* do not eavesdrop. It's only that, uh . . . I forgot my coat."

"You're wearing your coat," I said.

"I am *now*," Emma said.

"I can't help wondering," Mike said, "if Miss Howard might be hoping to damage my reputation, perhaps even get me fired, by telling everyone that I'm a ghost."

Clive gasped. *"Blackmail!"*

"Oh, puh-*leez*," Emma said. "I would *never*! Besides, it doesn't matter if you're queer or straight or trans or, uh . . . a ghost. The important thing is to be *your authentic self. That's* what they teach us in health class."

Mike nodded approval. "Health class has come a long way since I was a kid."

"There is, however, one *little* thing," Emma said.

Mike said, "Yes?"

Clive and I said, "Yes?"

"I don't love the new *Hamlet* script," she said, "which technically is the old *Hamlet* script. My parents say that *all* good stories have morals."

Mike said, "We're all entitled to wrong opinions, I suppose," which Emma, very busy expressing her own thoughts, must not have heard.

"*I* would never make a fuss," she continued. "It's *not* in my sweet nature. But I *was* thinking that if we go back to the original script, then *I* wouldn't have to tell Coach Fig and Mrs. Winklebottom and my parents and the entire town of Plattsfield about how *you* are delusional and *think* you are a ghost."

"Delusional?" Mike seemed hurt. "Miss Jessel, just to clarify, I *am* a ghost."

"Mr., uh . . . whatever your name is," Emma said.

"We all know there is *no such thing*. Ghosts are figments of overactive imaginations."

"Put another way, perhaps your imagination is underactive?" Mike said.

"*I* am not the problem here!" Emma said.

"Miss Jessel—Emma—*I* am neither unreasonable nor am I harsh, I hope. At the same time, I dislike having my credibility called to account. Put another way, what can I do to convince you?" Mike asked.

"Rattle some furniture?" I suggested.

Clive shook his head. "Oh no, that's okay, Mike. You don't need to . . ."

Mike himself did not move, but from behind us came *squeak-clatter-CLUMP, squeak-clatter-CLUMP*. Oh wow—the fifteen folding chairs seemed to be doing a waltz!

Emma glanced backstage and shrugged. "Big whoop," she said.

Mike's expression changed from hurt to annoyed.

Clive gulped, worried, like me, about what an annoyed ghost might do. I mean, he was Mike, the good guy who had volunteered to help with our play, but judging by movies and books and TV, ghosts were moody, and things could get ugly fast.

Then, bingo, a by-now-familiar chill wind propelled the curtains into flight and rattled invisible chains at the same time—the truly freaky part—a ghastly green lightning bolt zapped ceiling to stage and back again.

"*How about now? Do you believe I'm a ghost now?*" Mike asked, his words echoing like the voice of God in some old movie.

"I believe!" Clive said.

"Me too," I said.

Emma rolled her eyes. "Anyone can do sound effects."

"And this?" Mike asked, and then there were three Mikes, one on each side of the original, then five, and then seven, and then nine—each one translucent with a rainbow glow like a bubble, then—poof—they were gone and a single Mike remained, staring at Emma expectantly.

Emma tossed her hair. "So you used to work for Pixar or something."

Hands on hips, Clive turned to her. "Seriously? I mean, sure he could be some kind of engineering genius, but wa-a-ay more likely he's a ghost."

Emma did not bother to respond. I had one last idea. "Can you fly?" I asked Mike.

"With or without wings?" Mike said.

"With," Clive said.

"Eagle or angel?" Mike said.

"Angel," Clive said.

And like that, wings budded from Mike's shoulder blades, shredding his coat on their way to achieving pterodactyl span and sprouting clean white feathers. "Pretty good, right?" Mike looked over each shoulder to admire the effect, then bent his knees, flapped, and rose lightly over the boards.

What a sight! Like Gabriel himself ascending above Plattsfield-Winklebottom!

Only it didn't last long.

The wings were huge and unwieldy. Mike was not much of a pilot. Soon he'd gotten himself tangled in the rigging above the stage, and there he hung, flailing, unhappy, and stuck.

"Impressive," Emma said sarcastically.

"Do you need help?" I asked.

"I don't really like heights," Mike admitted.

"I'll get a ladder," Clive said, but before he could move, the big extension ladder from backstage came marching toward us—*clomp-clomp, clomp-clomp, clomp-clomp*—and stopped.

Without a word, I climbed to the second-highest

rung, leaned in, stretched my arm out, and tried to grab Mike's right ankle.

Only it wasn't there.

That is, his green-and-purple argyle sock was there. I could see it. I could feel the wool. But the warm flesh and bone that should have been beneath the ankle wasn't, and neither, when I tried to support him as he disentangled his wings from the ropes and wires, was the weight of a grown man. So what did I do?

I acted.

"Ready?" I asked Mike.

"Ready," he affirmed.

And rung by rung, hand clutching an ankle I could see but could not feel, I descended the ladder with weightless Mike poised at the end of my outstretched arm.

Clive applauded. "Better than the circus!"

Emma said, "Very nice," and, "I have to go. By tomorrow I expect the original script—Mrs. Winklebottom's script—will be back at rehearsal. Have a good evening, everybody." She made a flutter-finger wave, smiled to show off her teeth, and tripped away down the stairs to the house and out the lobby doors.

Mike's wings shrank to nothing. His coat fixed

itself. He dusted his shoulders and sighed. "Now, boys, I have a question. Which one of us is scarier?"

"Are you going to go back to the other script?" I asked.

"No," Mike said. "I will not give in to blackmail! I will not sacrifice Shakespeare for schlock!"

I started to explain to Clive about schlock, a Yiddish word my dad uses, but Clive said, "I *know*, Noah. You've been my friend since second grade."

"Sorry," I said. "But, Mike, if you don't cave, what will happen?"

"We'll have to quit, won't we?" Clive said. "And I was really getting into villainy, too."

"I don't know what will happen," Mike said.

"I thought ghosts could predict the future," I said.

Mike shook his head. "A lot of rules govern those of us in the afterlife. We cannot be seen by anyone who knew us when we were living; our appearance is always preceded by a warning wind; and each of us is called forth by unique incantation. As for seeing the future, that would require disruption of the space-time continuum. Not even a ghost has that much power."

CHAPTER NINETEEN

(SCENE: NOAH, MOM, and DAD at dinner that same evening.)

NOAH: Dad?

DAD *(chews, swallows, looks up)*: Yes, my son?

NOAH: What's the space-time continuum?

MOM: Hoo boy.

DAD *(looks at MOM, raises eyebrows)*: Aren't you glad your son is interested in what I do?

NOAH: Is that what you do, Dad? Space-time? Cool.

MOM: Your dad does lasers.

NOAH: Oh. Well. I guess lasers are cool.

DAD: Thank you.

NOAH: But you're a physicist. And space-time—you understand it? Sort of?

DAD: Of course I understand it. You see, Noah *(he settles in for a lengthy explanation)*—

MOM *(interrupting)*: Perhaps you could confine yourself to the thousand-word version?

NOAH *(looks back and forth between them)*: OMG, are
you guys still having that fight?

DAD: Your mother and I do not have fights.

MOM: Speak for yourself. I'm not over your crack
about science versus art. But we won't resolve it at
the dinner table. So I've declared a truce.

DAD: May I answer Noah's question now?

MOM: Five minutes. Tops.

DAD: So if he asks about, say, the poetry of Emily
Dickinson, do we also confine ourselves to five
minutes?

NOAH: Who's Emily Dickinson?

MOM: Funny you should ask. Emily Dickinson—

DAD: Wait a minute.

MOM: Only kidding. The space-time continuum.
(She puts her fork down.) I'm all ears.

DAD *(side-eyes MOM)*: Thank you. Most famously
described by Albert Einstein in his special theory
of relativity, the space-time continuum is the idea
that space and time are in fact part of the same
thing.

NOAH: Well, that's ridiculous. An inch is not the
same as a minute. *(He thinks.)* Is it?

DAD: Look at it this way. Up is not the same as down, but they both relate to where something is in space.

NOAH: Oka-a-ay.

DAD: So in space, there are three dimensions, correct? One dimension is a fixed point, two dimensions is back and forth—a line—and three dimensions adds depth—call it in and out.

NOAH: Fatness.

DAD *(thinks)*: Fatness.

DAD: So space-time adds a fourth dimension, call it *when.* Anything that exists, exists not only in space, but at a point or multiple points in time.

NOAH *(thinking)*: So then Abraham Lincoln not only existed in three dimensions in all the places he ever was, but he also existed from this date to that date, birth to death.

DAD *(looks at MOM)*: Boy's smarter than he looks.

MOM: Gets it from my side.

NOAH *(thoughtfully)*: So if someone existed for a while and ceased to exist—like, uh, died, then . . .

DAD: In a way, no one ever ceases to exist. Because everyone has a secure spot in space-time, which never ceases to exist but simply is.

NOAH: So we don't die!

MOM: Except—

DAD: Killjoy.

MOM: Except that our consciousness, our awareness, is limited by the biology of our senses. So just as we can't see the past, we can't see the dead, even if they're all around us. Our human eyes and ears and sense of touch, they're not, uh . . . *enabled* for those purposes, which may not be a bad thing. It would be overwhelming to constantly navigate a maze of ghosts.

NOAH: Tell me about it. So, in other words, ghosts might be real.

DAD *(puts down fork, shakes head emphatically)*: Wait just a minute. Your mother and I never intended to say that ghosts are real.

MOM *(annoyed)*: I can speak for myself, thank you, and I am not so sure. Think of thunder and lightning, night and day, the phases of the moon, Noah. Science explains them now, but once they seemed like magic.

NOAH: So maybe it's the same with ghosts?

MOM: Sure. Maybe science just hasn't gotten around to explaining ghosts yet.

DAD: Nonsense.

CHAPTER TWENTY

Thursday, Rehearsal Week Two, 36 Days till Performance

I got to school early the next morning and, like I expected, found Emma by herself at her usual table in the caf. When the weather is good, which in Plattsfield means the first two weeks of school and the last two weeks of school, people wait outside for the bell in the morning. The rest of the time, people hang inside.

Emma was almost always in the caf early because her parents dropped her off before work and, as she made sure to tell everybody, they were both attorneys and got to their office at practically *dawn* so they could help the people of Plattsfield get divorced, fight with relatives about money, and sue neighbors over barking dogs and tree branches.

That last part isn't according to Emma; it's according to my parents.

I swung my butt onto the bench at Emma's table. She looked up, surprised, but then she turned pink a little and smiled that bright smile, which was weird. I was furious at her, and here she was looking like she was glad to see me.

"We're going back to the other script, right?" she said. "Mike realizes it's for the best?"

"No," I said. "We're not and he doesn't and besides, you know what will happen if you tell people that Mike's a ghost?"

"*Thinks* he's a ghost," Emma said. "The man is probably dangerous."

"A danger to you? Or me? Or the Plattsfield-Winklebottom Memorial Sixth-Grade Players? We seem to be doing a great job taking care of ourselves so far. Anyway, if he's delusional, so am I, and so is Clive, and if you tell everybody he's a ghost, then people will freak out, and Coach Fig will have to take over, and there will be no Plattsfield-Winklebottom Memorial Sixth-Grade Play this year, and it will be your fault. Did you think of that?"

Emma tossed her hair, then proceeded to ignore

all my very good points. "Who *is* he anyway? The ghost of *who?*"

"He's the ghost of . . . uh . . . Mike," I said. "Mike who knows a lot about Shakespeare and plays. Mike who is teaching us a lot about Shakespeare and drama. Mike who is going to make sure there is a show this year, which Fig is too busy to do. *That* Mike."

"Uh-huh, and how do I know he's not *dangerous?*"

"Are you even listening?" I raised my voice. She raised hers. We went around again, stuck in a circle, until I, Noah McNichol, had a genius idea.

"Emma . . . ," I said, quieting down.

"What?"

"What if I find out who he is—who he was? Then would you agree not to rat him out?"

"How are you going to do that?" she asked.

"Uh . . . *ask* him?" I said.

"Ha! He very cleverly refused to tell us his last name, remember? And anyway, how would you know he was telling the truth?"

"So I'll think of something," I said. "And when I do, and he turns out to be harmless, you agree to keep quiet about the ghost stuff. Deal?"

Emma didn't say anything. She was thinking.

"Give me a couple of weeks," I said. "If I haven't

identified Mike by then, you can do what you want."

"Problem!" Emma cried. "In a couple of weeks, it will be too late. We'll have the script memorized. We won't be able to change back."

"Yeah, we will," I said. "The costumes and sets are the same, and the old script, the No-Trauma one, is way shorter. We can learn it in no time. At least, *I* can. Maybe not you. Maybe you're not that good at memorizing."

"Are you saying I'm dumb?"

"I'm saying two weeks."

Emma huffed and puffed some more, which I got. It's totally her personality. She had to show she'd never really surrender. At last she said, "All right, but after that—"

"After that, tell whoever you want—Mrs. Winkle-bottom, your parents, the cast, the TV stations, public radio for all I care. Till then, we have a deal."

Lunch was the kind of flat grilled cheese sandwich that glues your tongue to the roof of your mouth and tastes like salty grease. A caf classic.

Clive and I sat together at a table away from the drama geeks. I had decided to avoid Emma till I was ready to make my report.

"If Emma tells everybody . . . ," Clive began as

soon as we sat down. "Tenantless graves! Stars with trains of fire! Disasters in the sun!"

"Act one," I said. "And I got this."

"Good," Clive said. "Because I like playing Claudius the way he is in the real script, a bad, bad dude. 'O, my offence is rank. It smells to heaven. It hath the primal eldest curse upon't. *A brother's murder.*'"

Clive was dropping his *R*s like he had some English accent, and when he said *bruthuh's muhduh*, he leaned in close so I could smell the fruit punch on his breath.

Creepy.

"Do you *mind*?" I shoved him aside.

"I know, right? My mom thinks it's alarming to have me in the house. She's afraid I'll mix poison in the bathroom sink and pour it in the cat's ear for practice."

"Would you do that?" I asked.

"Of course not. Probably," Clive said. "So, uh . . . you got this, but may I ask exactly how?"

I told him about my deal with Emma. Then I revealed my plan to learn Mike's identity, which I had come up with instead of taking notes on the Ming dynasty. It was clever, elaborate, made up of many moving parts, not to mention it required a Sherlock Holmes hat and a magnifying glass and an ample supply of pancakes.

Okay, not really.

In fact, it was simple. IRL Mike had been someone who knew about theater, about directing, about Shakespeare. His clothes looked like they were from the eighties maybe. He might've been a professor like my mom. Or he might've been an actor or a director, on Broadway even, but not famous. I mean, none of us Sixth-Grade Players recognized him, right? He couldn't be famous.

Anyway, in Plattsfield there were two people who really knew theater. One was Mrs. Winklebottom, and I couldn't talk to her.

The other was Miss Magnus, and here was my plan: pay her a visit, pet the chihuahua, ask polite questions, and with great subtlety and keenness, see if she could identify Mike.

There was a slight chance this might not work. But at least it was a start.

I had barely explained all this when I noticed Fuli coming from the food line with her tray, searching for a place to sit.

I looked at Clive. He nodded. I waved. "Hey, Prince Hamlet—sit with us. Plenty of room."

Fuli came over, sat, opened her carton of milk, put her napkin in her lap. "Don't you usually sit at the drama table?" she asked.

"We've been exiled," I said, which was a lie but sounded appropriately dramatic.

"Ostracized," Clive agreed.

"Relegated to outsider status," I said.

Fuli took a small, tidy bite and chewed it thoroughly. "'Relegated'? Such a big word."

"His parents are professors," Clive said, "in case you didn't know. And Emma's are lawyers."

"*Attorneys,*" I clarified. "And don't compare me to her, please."

"Why this relegation?" Fuli asked. "I would not call either of you an outsider."

"Sure I am. I'm the Black kid," Clive said. "Half Black. Look around. Sea of white faces. Do you see any more like me?"

"And I am the Asian," Fuli said, "the girl with the dumplings. And by the way, Clive, I bet my skin is as dark as yours."

"No way," Clive said.

Fuli rolled up her sleeve. "Compare."

Clive rolled up his sleeve, laid his arm on the table next to Fuli's. Sure enough, two arms, one color.

"Hey, talk about ostracized," I said. "I may be pale-skinned, but I'm Jewish, and, uh . . . my arm has freckles."

"What do you say, Clive?" Fuli asked. "Shall we let him be an outsider too?"

"I guess," Clive said, "honorary status. And we could invite Diego. He's another one of us brown ones."

"Where does he go at lunch, anyway?" I asked.

"No one knows," Clive said.

"I do," Fuli said. "Art room. Ms. Mock lets him fool around on the fancy computer, the one with all the graphics stuff. She thinks he's some kind of artistic genius ever since he made that collage with rat teeth."

Even I knew about that collage. Diego had made it in fourth grade, and he and Ms. Mock both got in trouble with the principal for a while, but then my parents and some of the other university types defended them, and the trouble went away. Tempest in a teapot, my dad would say. Still, it had been a big deal at the time.

Clive said, "For real, Fuli. You can't call yourself an outsider anymore. You got cast as Hamlet."

"Don't remind me!" I said, all drama, and Clive shoved me, and I shoved him back, and Fuli ignored us and kept eating.

"Seriously?" Clive went on. "What could be more inside than Hamlet, Prince of Denmark?"

Fuli drank her last sip of milk, wiped her mouth with her napkin, refolded it, set it on her tray. She looked at Clive, looked at me. "All right, if you say so, I am an insider. But I still don't have a place to sit at lunch."

Fuli wasn't trying to be dramatic, I don't think. She was stating a fact. Still, I felt a twinge in my heart, and I guarantee so did Clive. All those episodes of *Gossip Girl*, right?

"You do now, Fuli," I said. "Anytime."

CHAPTER TWENTY-ONE

(SCENE: *Dining room, early evening. NOAH, DAD, and MOM are eating dinner.*)

DAD: How's the play going, Noah? How was rehearsal today? How's that odd director you've told us about . . . ? Matt, is it?

MOM and NOAH: Mike!

DAD: That's it. Mike. He wears a fedora or a porkpie or a Stetson or a Yankees cap . . . and he is somewhat mysterious.

NOAH (*hastily*): Wait—mysterious? Says who?

DAD (*taken aback*): Uh, you?

NOAH: No, no, Dad. He's perfectly normal. Ordinary. Usual. Forget I said anything different and, uh . . . today's rehearsal? It was good. We blocked the whole thing with the ghost in act one and, oh, another big thing—this kid Justin sprained his shoulder and can't play baseball, so he's doing lights and sound and all that from the booth. Mike calls that job holy spirit—you know, because of "let there be light"?

DAD: Funny guy.

MOM: And how is Fuli doing as Hamlet? Are you still smarting about that?

DAD and NOAH: "Smarting"?

MOM (*sheepishly*): So I'm old, Father William, and in my youth we said "smarting." It means are you still sad that you didn't get the part?

NOAH: Nah, I'm over it.

(*MOM and DAD trade sympathetic looks. NOAH busily spoons baked beans.*)

NOAH (*swallows, mumbling*): She's doing okay. (*He looks up, speaks up.*) Actually, she's doing a lot more than okay. She's kind of amazing. I mean, I'm boffo and all, but I never could have done such a good job. Mike calls it range—charming in one speech and whack the next, but she always makes it seem natural.

DAD: She is mad north by northwest then—boom!— she knows a hawk from a handsaw.

MOM (*frowns*): Act two . . . I think?

DAD: Paraphrasing.

NOAH: Yeah, act two, and sheesh, Dad, for someone who hates theater, you really know your *Hamlet*.

DAD: I don't hate—

MOM: It seems to me you enjoy talking about the play and the rehearsals.

DAD: I enjoy lasers, too.

MOM: So there's room in that big brain of yours for both.

DAD *(pats head)*: It is rather a big brain, isn't it?

(MOM and NOAH make gagging sounds)

NOAH: So speaking of theater, I have a question. You know Miss Magnus, right? Do you know where she lives? I tried to look it up, but I couldn't find an address.

MOM: Somebody at Sal's will if I ask.

DAD: Who's Miss Magnus?

MOM *(looks at the ceiling)*: Oh, sweet heaven, I sometimes wonder if we all live in the same house in the same town or what. *(She looks at DAD.)* Don't you ever stop thinking of laser beams and muons?

DAD: Not often. And so I repeat: Who's Miss Magnus?

NOAH: The real director? Who broke her leg on Broadway? Basically a legend at my school? That Miss Magnus?

MOM: A legend?

NOAH: She works seriously hard. One year she stayed up all night sewing sequins onto Juliet's wedding gown.

MOM *(after a beat)*: Wedding gown? In *Romeo and Juliet?*

NOAH: At the end. You know, when Romeo and Juliet get married.

DAD: No-Trauma Drama strikes again.

NOAH: That's not the real ending? Let me guess—in Shakespeare's version, everybody dies.

MOM: Not quite everybody.

DAD: Only Romeo and Juliet.

MOM: And Mercutio.

DAD: And Tybalt.

MOM: I think the nurse survives.

DAD: No wonder I hate theater.

MOM: We're not starting that again.

DAD: We're not. But do you mean the Miss Magnus who lives over on Beekman?

(Astonished, NOAH and MOM look at DAD, who takes a bite, chews in a self-satisfied manner, looks from one to the other.)

NOAH *(recovers, sets fork down)*: But how—

MOM: Yes. How?

DAD: Her niece was one of my TAs last year. So I think of Miss Magnus as Samantha's aunt, not a legend, but I believe I have it right. I knew she taught something.

NOAH: Where on Beekman?

DAD: I don't know the house number, Noah. Sheesh. I only remember at all because I ran into Samantha and she was rushing off to walk her aunt's chihuahua.

NOAH: That's Miss Magnus, all right.

DAD: I can get the house number from Samantha if you want.

NOAH: That would be great.

MOM: But why do you want to know?

NOAH *(ready for this, piously)*: Poor, poor Miss Magnus. I feel so bad for her stuck indoors with her broken leg. I just thought she might like company. *(He sighs sadly.)*

(MOM and DAD look at NOAH skeptically.)

DAD: Touching. But not credible.

NOAH *(hurt)*: You don't believe me?

MOM: And neither do I.

NOAH *(fist to heart)* : Can't I do a nice thing without being questioned and doubted all the time? Is that too much to ask?

(DAD and MOM look at each other quizzically, seem to come to an agreement.)

DAD: You're overacting, Noah.

MOM: Even so, whatever you're up to, I can't see that it's too terrible. Besides, Miss Magnus probably could use company.

CHAPTER TWENTY-TWO

I gave myself two weeks to save the day.

I should have made it three.

First, I was busy rehearsing and memorizing lines for four separate characters.

Four!!!

Take that, Fuli, who only has to play Hamlet, and Clive, who thinks he's some kind of a big deal because he gets to be the villain.

After that—*boom*—it was Passover.

For the memorizing, I gave up playing *ShredSauce* and stayed awake an extra half hour every night, which, when you think about it, that's *commitment to my art* right there.

Once I started to get the hang, Mom helped me run lines. She was good in the scene in the graveyard.

There's a part where Hamlet is talking to a skull and I, Gravedigger One, am hanging around along with Hamlet's friend Horatio.

It was Saturday afternoon, and we were at the kitchen table. There were no skulls available, so Mom took a green apple from the bowl, looked at it sadly, and said, "'Alas, poor Yorick! I knew him, Horatio.'" And when the speech goes on—"'Where be your gibes now? Your gambols? Your songs?'"—Mom's voice caught, and she got tears in her eyes.

"Whoa, you're really into this," I said.

Mom sniffed. "I don't see that line anywhere in the script, Noah."

"Oh, sorry. I mean, it's great that you're into it. But IRL—are you okay, Mom?"

"I'm fine. I was"—she sniffed again—"thinking about my dad."

"Did Grandpa like apples?"

That made her smile. "Funny guy. Like your father. And mine, too, I guess, because gibes and gambols— jokes and pranks—make me think of him."

My grandfather died last year, some kind of heart something. He was fine, and then my grandmother called, and then Mom was crying and Dad was hugging her, and then we were on a plane to California for the service. That's where those grandparents lived; when we visited them we'd go to Disneyland and Universal and the beach.

They never visited us. They didn't like the climate, they said.

I was sad my grandfather was dead, mostly sad for my grandmother because now she was by herself. But for real? My grandfather had never been part of my everyday life. It was rare for me to think about him. Now I saw for my mom it was different.

"They talk about death a lot in *Hamlet*. Did you notice?" I asked Mom.

"I noticed," Mom said. "And Claudius says since death is natural, you shouldn't be too sad. ''Tis a fault to heaven,' if you are."

"I know," I said, "but Claudius is the villain, don't forget. It's not like you can trust him for good advice."

As for Passover, that was the next week, and my other grandparents came, my dad's mom—I call her Gigi—and her husband, Ted. Ted is Husband No. 6, according to Dad, but he's Husband No. 5, according to Mom. This is a joke in our family, the point being that Gigi has had enough husbands my parents can't keep track.

The last one, Arnie, was nice and shiny-bald and had a flattened nose because once he was in a fight. I didn't know any of the husbands before that. The first one must've been my dad's real father—biological, I mean—and the second was Mr. McNichol.

Mom explained all about this to me once, but since then I forgot.

Gigi and Ted flew into the airport in Montreal. Dad drove to pick them up. I took the next day off school, but I still went to rehearsal. As Clive would say: *priorities.*

That afternoon Coach Fig put in an appearance, wearing his headset as usual. He must've been between phone calls because when he spoke it was to us, the people with him in the same room. At first nobody answered, it was so unexpected.

"Everything okay here?" he asked, looking around the bare stage. "Say, Mike, not to tell you your business, but shouldn't we be ordering up some plywood and paint? Maybe looking out for costume donations? I've got emails from some o' the parents and they'd be delighted to step in and help."

Mike opened his mouth to answer, but Fig raised a finger, cocked his head, looked into the great faraway. "Yes? This is he . . . Mother Mary, are you serious! What can possibly be bad about fruit salad?"

And away he walked.

"Good to see you, Coach." Mike spoke to Fig's retreating back. "And never fear, I've got it under control."

But did he? In actual fact, we'd all noticed there was no set, not even a throne or a headstone or an arras, which is, like, the Shakespeare word for "curtain." Polonius is hiding behind one, spying on Hamlet and his mother, Gertrude, when Hamlet stabs through it with a sword and kills him by mistake.

Emma played Polonius, remember, and this was her favorite part of the show. Polonius never shut up, which meant Emma had to memorize loads of lines. In the scene when Polonius died, she made a horrible *gag-gurgle* sound and squealed, "Oh! I am slain!" and fell down so hard she went *thud.*

You know Emma is less than my favorite person, but when it came to Polonius, she really inhabited the character. One day Diego—he was wearing a grass-green beret—actually burst into applause when she was done dying: "Heck yeah!"

The Sunday after Passover, Dad drove Gigi and Ted back to the airport. It happened to be Easter, a cheap day to fly, which is one of the perks of being Jewish.

Before my grandparents left, our house was all buzzing with activity: hugs and kisses (from Gigi); pats on the back and "Be good, my boy!" (from Ted); my mother dashing from this bathroom to another, holding up bottles of lotion and shampoo and saying: "Is this yours? What about this one? I'm sure it isn't mine."

Finally, Dad ushered the company out the door, and Mom took a grateful breath, then—*whoosh*—the door opened, and they were back, all three of them. Gigi thought she had forgotten her phone. More thumping on the stairs, more questions:

"Where did you have it last?"

"Bottom of the closet?"

"Laundry basket?"

It was in her purse.

They left again. Mom sighed again. Mom went upstairs and, a half second later, *thump-thump*ed down, threw open the front door, and dashed barefoot into the street waving the keys to Ted's Cadillac. She was breathing hard when she came back, flashed me a thumbs-up, and dropped onto the sofa.

Visits from relatives are pretty overwhelming, but you get used to having them around. Suddenly the house felt quiet.

Then I noticed something. "Uh-oh. Did they leave that, too?"

Mom looked at the coffee table, where I was pointing. There lay a dusty book—scrapbook-size, beat-up, covered in crinkly black leather.

"That they left on purpose, your Gigi did," Mom said. "Family photographs or something. Your dad wanted nothing to do with them. Gigi thought maybe you'd take a look sometime."

I wasn't busy, so sure, why not? I started across the room, but my phone buzzed: Clive. Did I want to come over for his family's egg hunt in the afternoon? Beaucoup candy to be had.

I'm Jewish, I texted back.

The Easter Bunny says that's okay, Clive answered.

I responded with a thumbs-up. Then I asked my mom and headed upstairs to get ready, forgetting all about the dusty book.

CHAPTER TWENTY-THREE

Monday, Rehearsal Week Four, 25 Days till Performance

Dad got Miss Magnus's address from his ex-TA Samantha the same day Mom got it from the checker at Sal's.

"Here you go, son," Dad said, handing me the address, 1750 Beekman, on a slip of paper when he picked me up at school. "Hope it helps you out."

Mom gave me the same address in ink on the back of a Sal's receipt in the kitchen a few minutes later. "I think you were looking for this?" she said.

I thanked them both and never let on I'd gotten the intel twice. Somehow, Miss Magnus's address had become part of the parentals' battle about art versus science. I've lived in this family eleven long years. For the sake of harmony, I knew it would be better if each one thought they'd notched a victory.

Meanwhile, I had another problem.

I couldn't just show up at 1750 Beekman. Wouldn't that be rude?

So after dinner I texted Clive, who is polite, and he said, "Write Miss Magnus an email," and then—having friends can be helpful—he even found the email address after consulting with his big sister, Gillian, who had it in her contacts because once she'd been a Plattsfield-Winklebottom Memorial Sixth-Grade Player herself.

Gillian's year they did *Macbeth, Tale of a Happy Marriage.*

I sent the email from the dinosaur computer in the basement, which seemed appropriate because Miss Magnus is not so young herself. First, I thought for a while about grammar and spelling, because when Miss Magnus wasn't directing, she taught English, and then I typed this:

Hello, Miss Magnus,
I would like to come and see you to discuss a
matter of importance relating to the Plattsfield-
Winklebottom Memorial Sixth-Grade Play.
Is that okay?
How about Wednesday after school, when we
don't have rehearsal?

Sincerely,
Noah McNichol
Plattsfield-Winklebottom Memorial Sixth Grader

I hit send and waited. And waited. And decided to do my math homework (graphs) because it was possible Miss Magnus did not spend every moment sitting by her computer anticipating urgent emails from Noah McNichol.

"Noah?" my mom called a few minutes later. "Time to abandon screens for the day and brush your teeth! Noah?"

"Coming!"

My math was done. I checked my email one last time, and—*hooray*—found this:

Dear Noah,
Wednesday would be fine. I will make tea.
Sincerely,
Janet Magnus
Erstwhile Director, Plattsfield-Winklebottom
Memorial Sixth-Grade Players
PS I hope you are not allergic to chihuahuas.

CHAPTER TWENTY-FOUR

Wednesday, Rehearsal Week Four, 22 Days till Performance

The day I walked from school to Miss Magnus's house was the first warm one that spring.

By warm, I mean Plattsfield warm, over fifty degrees and drippy. Still, a few daring crocuses showed their colors on marshy lawns and in flower beds, and a kid could almost imagine the day it would be summer and he'd be wearing flip-flops instead of boots, a ball cap instead of a beanie.

Number 1750 was in the middle of the block, a house smaller than mine with yellow wood siding and blue trim, a covered porch, and a shuttered front window overlooking the lawn. Under the window was a flower bed where maybe there'd be zinnias like at our house in summer, even though now it was nothing but dead gray stems and mud.

I stood on the front porch. I took a breath. I rang

the bell. I hoped there would be cookies. I wondered why the famous chihuahua didn't bark. Had something terrible happened to him?

Of course I'd seen Miss Magnus around school, but she'd never been my teacher. I didn't know her except for the legend part. If something had happened to her dog, she might be in a bad mood, might not want to answer questions.

And then what would I do?

A voice called, "Come in, Noah. It's open."

I opened the door to a house much more jumbly than mine, full of what Gigi would call gimcrackery: photos and paintings in fancy frames, books on every table, little statues—figurines, I guess—on dark wood shelves.

Miss Magnus sat in a stuffed tan chair near the cold fireplace. Her legs rested on a red footstool, the left one bound in a brace. Next to her on the floor was a basket, and in the basket lay the chihuahua, which raised its head and looked around but could not be bothered either to locate the disturbance (me) or to bark.

"He's not much of a watchdog anymore," Miss Magnus said. Then, "You must be Noah. I hope you don't mind if I don't get up."

"Hey, hi, yeah," I said, took three strides across the small room, clasped her outstretched hand. "Noah, that's me. It's nice to meet you and, uh"—I looked down at the dog, who appeared to be snoozing—"him, too."

"His name is Ducat," she said.

"No way! Like 'dead for a ducat, dead'?" The dog looked up. Was he frowning? "No offense," I said.

"I named him because as a puppy he was small and gold. I wasn't thinking one day it might seem morbid," she said.

I bobbed my head yes, then realized I was being over-the-top charming and eager. Maybe I should dial it back a bit, as Mike might say.

I took a breath and, trying not to be too obvious about it, studied Miss Magnus herself—small for a grown-up, not much bigger than me; white with straight brown hair and bangs; big, slightly anxious smile. She was wearing red earrings and pink-framed glasses and a caftan, which I know the word for because Gigi wears caftans around the condo. Miss Magnus's had diamond shapes and squares all over it.

On the table beside her was a book called *Contemporary Poems for the Naughty and Nice*. I was embarrassed when she noticed me looking, but she only said, "Ducat likes the naughty ones best." She added, "The tea tray is in the kitchen, if you don't mind bringing it in."

I found the kitchen, found the tray on the counter set up with a carafe of tea, two mugs, sugar, cream, and—yay!—a plate of cookies.

"Do you mind pouring out?" she asked. "Sorry to be so lame—ha ha. Literally. I hobbled around getting things ready, and now the busted leg is feeling it."

"Oh, I'm sorry," I said, hoping I wouldn't spill tea everywhere. "I didn't mean you should go to any trouble."

"I'm glad to do it. The PT—physical therapist—says I'm supposed to put weight on my leg. Besides, it's nice to be civilized on occasion. We really ought to have cups and saucers, not mugs, but this was the best I could do. Now, take a seat. I think there's room on the love seat if you just move over those old *Playbills*."

Tea is not bad with sugar in it. The cookies were crunchy with icing on top. Miss Magnus asked how the play was going, how my school year was going, and did I prefer skiing or snowboarding because in her experience sixth graders in Plattsfield had strong preferences one way or the other. She was easy to talk to, but that made sense. Talking to kids was her job.

"Now," she said, when the cookie plate was empty and so was my mug. "What is this 'matter of importance'? How can I help you?"

CHAPTER TWENTY-FIVE

had known Miss Magnus would ask this, of course. I had practiced my answer with Clive so I'd get the wording right, not give anything away. Miss Magnus might be a legend, but she was also a grown-up. If she thought I was asking about the guy helping Fig out with *Hamlet*, if she thought there was something strange, she'd go straight to Mrs. Winklebottom, and Emma would have succeeded, and bye-bye-the-show-must-go-on.

"I'm trying to identify somebody. He knows a lot about theater. He might be a director. His first name is Mike."

"All ri-i-i-ight," Miss Magnus said, taking this in. "Do you have a photograph?"

I shook my head. "There were, uh . . . technical difficulties." At rehearsal, Clive and I had tried three times to sneak a photo of Mike. Snapping one without anybody noticing is hard. Snapping one of a ghost turns out to be impossible, even with Clive's way-superior-to-mine phone. Twice, where Mike should have been, there was only a blobby blur.

The third time there was a grinning skeleton labeled RIP MIKE.

Funny guy.

"And why is it you want to know this person's identity?" Miss Magnus asked.

I was ready for that one, too. "Homework," I said. When you're dealing with a teacher, "homework" is all-purpose, right? Every teacher believes in homework.

"This must be a very unusual assignment," Miss Magnus said. "Whose class is it?"

"Oh, you don't know him . . . her, I mean," I said.

"I don't? I've been at Plattsfield-Winklebottom Memorial a long time."

"This teacher is new," I said. "Like, really new."

"Oh—you mean the gentleman who's helping Coach Newton with *Hamlet*? But he can't be assigning homework, can he? You've got plenty to do to get your lines down."

"Not him!" I said. "Definitely not him! It's . . . a

girl, a woman, a *sub.* And she brought in this guy, see, and introduced him as someone with a background in theater, and he talked to us for a little while, and then she gave us the assignment of figuring out who he is."

Clive and I had worked all this out in advance, of course. Convincing, right? Also, I was smiling my biggest, most boffo smile.

Never mind ratcheting it down.

Miss Magnus looked skeptical.

"What else do you know about this Mike? Approximately how old is he?" she asked.

"How old does he look, you mean?"

Miss Magnus knit her brows, puzzled, then smiled. "Ah yes. I see. If he's in the theater, it's likely he's had work done—plastic surgery—and he may look much younger than he is. But take a guess."

"Not really young. His hair is almost white," I said.

Miss Magnus tugged a lock of her own brown hair. "Doesn't color it. Well, typically a person doesn't go gray till their midforties anyway. Fat? Thin? Race? What about wrinkles?"

"Thin, pretty tall. Wrinkles around his eyes and frown lines on his forehead. He's white and, oh, does this help? I think he's Jewish."

Miss Magnus raised her eyebrows. "All right. But why do you think that?"

"He has a Star of David pin on his . . . what's it called? Lapel?"

"I see." Miss Magnus nodded. "Perhaps that does narrow it down. Unusually handsome? Movie-star handsome?"

I shook my head. "No, but not ugly or anything."

"So an average-looking white man in his sixties, most likely Jewish. How was he dressed?"

"Different," I said, then hesitated, afraid again I might give too much away. On the other hand, if I told her his clothes were old-fashioned, it's not like she'd jump to the conclusion he's a ghost. "Do you know that movie *It's a Wonderful Life*? Clive—he's my best friend—his family is into old movies, so I watch it with them at Christmastime, even though I'm Jewish."

"Jewish like your mystery man," Miss Magnus said.

"Is that a clue?"

"We will take it under consideration," she said. "And I've seen *It's a Wonderful Life* a hundred times, so I understand about his attire. Now tell me this: How do you know he was involved in theater?"

"Well, that's what the teacher, the *sub*, told us, like

I said. But besides, there's the way he talks," I said. "He, uh . . . mentioned directing, like maybe he's done it before. And, uh, he mentioned how import- ant art is, real art, not the No-Trauma Drama kind."

Miss Magnus's hands were folded in her lap. Now she looked down at them. "You're shaming me, Noah. I never liked those scripts. But Mrs. Winkle- bottom was the boss. I did what I could, hoped my sixth graders would catch the theater bug, find the real plays for themselves one day."

I felt bad. "I didn't mean to shame you, Miss Magnus."

"Never mind. Perhaps I should have fought harder. Perhaps I will next year. As for your mysterious Mike, I have an idea. If he has a career in theater, he might be quite accomplished, and still you wouldn't recog- nize him."

"I thought of that, too," I said.

"You see that pile of old *Playbill*s beside you on the love seat?"

I never heard of *Playbill*, but I saw a stack of mag- azines with that title on the cover, pulled one off the top, and saw it was actually the program for *Wicked,* a famous show I want like anything to see. Looking at the others, I saw they were programs, too.

"Have you seen every one of these shows?" I asked Miss Magnus.

She nodded. "I save the *Playbill* as a souvenir. I'm afraid I have piles of the things all over the house. These are all from the early 2000s. I pulled them out thinking this is my chance to get organized, but I got distracted, started reading them instead."

I thumbed through the *Playbill* for *Wicked*, then one for *Hairspray*, and another for *Newsies*. All of them had tiny photos of the cast and the director, sometimes of the tech crew as well.

Miss Magnus shifted in her chair, efficient all of a sudden. "You take the rest of the ones on the love seat. And I'll start with a stack from the shelf. We don't have much to go on, but maybe something you said will jog my memory."

There were a lot of *Playbill*s, and in each one a lot of photos. From math class I knew that a lot times a lot equals a ton, and it would therefore take a ton of time for me to search. I didn't have a better idea, but after a while—and no sign of Mike—I wished I hadn't drunk quite so much tea.

"Uh . . . Miss Magnus?" I looked up.

"Off the kitchen to the right," she said without looking up.

Whoa—just like when Mike read my mind!

Was Miss Magnus a ghost, too?

Hoo boy, Noah, buddy. Get a grip.

When I came back, Miss Magnus had marked three potential Mikes. One was a stage manager, one a lighting designer, and one a director.

"I think these guys are all too young," I said.

Miss Magnus cocked her head. "But these photos were taken twenty years ago. These Mikes would be in their fifties or sixties now."

"Ye-e-e-e-es," I said, "but, uh . . . I think my Mike is *very* well preserved."

Miss Magnus made a face. If she ran out of patience with me—and who could blame her—I would have to go to plan B.

Whatever that was.

But then, at last, I got lucky.

Miss Magnus was staring at the *Playbill* for a play called *Waiting for Godot,* which starred Robin Williams, the guy from that old movie *Hook.* "Hmmm," she said. "Here's another possibility. He is Jewish, escaped Nazi Germany as a child, in fact. But there's one slight problem."

She didn't say anything more, just handed me the program. The name of the play's director was Mike

Einstein. I flipped the page, and there was the tiny photo and—even though he was much younger and wearing black-frame glasses—it was absolutely Mike.

"That's him!" I said. "We did it! What's the problem?"

But I knew the answer before the question was out of my mouth.

"Mike Einstein is dead," she said.

That was the moment I realized maybe Clive and I hadn't entirely thought this through.

"He had a twin?" I tried.

"Also named Mike?" Miss Magnus said.

"Parents lacked imagination?"

"Hmmm," Miss Magnus said.

"Well, uh . . . if we could just forget for a sec that this Mike Einstein fellow is dead . . . what do you know about him?" I asked.

"Mike Einstein? Well! He's only the best Broadway director of the twentieth century," Miss Magnus said. "That is, to begin with."

"But . . . ," I said, doubtful, "I never heard of him."

"Noah?" Miss Magnus said. "Can you name any Broadway directors?"

I thought for a sec and couldn't.

"Fans know actors and occasionally playwrights.

Only the most devoted know the directors," Miss Magnus said. "But I still don't see how . . . ?"

Uh-oh. I'd found out what I wanted to know, and I was super grateful to Miss Magnus, I was. But now I had one more quick question, and then it was time to exit stage pronto.

"This Mike Einstein guy, he wasn't *dangerous,* was he? I mean to people or sixth graders or anything?"

Miss Magnus raised her eyebrows. "Dangerous? Not that I ever heard. His reputation was excellent, but if he's dead, how could he—"

I was on my feet. "'More things in heaven and earth'?" I tried. And then I had a brainstorm. "Does Ducat need a walk? I can take him out for you."

"Oh, Noah. How nice. Yes, I'd appreciate that and so would he, wouldn't you, Ducat?"

Ducat looked up, looked at me. There might have been gratitude in those watery old eyes. I couldn't tell.

"His harness is hanging by the front door. Do you mind getting it? And I'll do the buckles."

Walking Ducat didn't take long. The poor guy was really eager for relief, if you know what I mean. Soon he was settling back in his basket and Miss Magnus was thanking me again.

"No problem. Thank *you*. You've been super help-ful. *Super* helpful." I scooted toward the door fast, talking my head off to avoid questions. "So, you'll be at the show, right? It'll be great to see you again. So great."

Miss Magnus shook her head. "If my leg's better, I'm planning a little trip. I'm afraid if I were in the audience, I'd only second-guess Coach Newton and his assistant. And that wouldn't do anyone any good. But, Noah—"

"All righty, then." My hand was on the doorknob. I was turning the doorknob. I was pulling the door. I was making my escape. "I mean, uh, that's too bad. Seriously. But I'll see you around, I bet. Thanks again. A lot. Goodbye!"

Exit to front stoop, wipe pretend sweat from brow, silently *whoop* for joy. Mission accomplished! Deed done!

Noah McNichol saves the day!

CHAPTER TWENTY-SIX

started to text Clive on my walk home, then changed my mind and called. I was eager to bask in my well-deserved glory.

He picked up first ring. "What happened?"

"I ate her whole plate of cookies," I told him. "It was embarrassing, but I was hungry because—"

"Noah!" Clive interrupted. "I have no time for Miss Magnus's cookies! Yes or no—did you find out who Mike is? Was?"

"Yes," I said, then I told him, then there was a pause while he digested this amazing news.

Finally, Clive said, "I am being directed by one of the best Broadway directors ever?"

"This isn't about you, Clive," I said.

"Heck it's not. I feel special. Only—"

"Only what?"

"Only *why*? Of all the gin joints in all the world, why did he walk into ours?"

I guessed I was supposed to know what Clive was talking about, only I didn't, and I walked all the way to the corner trying to puzzle it out so I wouldn't have to show my ignorance by asking.

It was no use.

"Noah? Earth to Noah?" Clive said. "Do you need me to explain the reference?"

"Is 'gin joint' from *Gossip Girl*?" I asked.

"Not from *Gossip Girl*. It means a bar, dummy. Where they sell gin. It's from the movie *Casablanca*. The amount of culture you lack is sometimes stunning."

"Uh-huh, and I'm your biggest fan, too."

"Humphrey Bogart says it to Ingrid Bergman."

"Whoever they are. What's your point?" I had stopped walking, was standing on the corner of Oneida and Beekman. The sun was descending toward the western hills, turning the evening sky pink.

"So in the movie, Bergman is Bogart's old girl-friend, and he owns this bar in the town of Casa-blanca, see, and out of nowhere she shows up one day . . ."

I started walking again. I fiddled with my jacket. To zip or not to zip? Two blocks and I'd be home. "Uh-huh."

"And he says something like, 'Of all the gin joints in all the world, you walk into mine.'"

I gave up on zipping, tried to take in what Clive was telling me. "Gin joints are bars, you said. So the point?"

"It's an amazing coincidence!" Clive said. "Mike the superstar could be helping out any drama club anywhere, a way better one than ours. Why is he here?"

By now I was two front yards from my own and, I don't mind saying, I was ticked. Didn't I deserve congratulations? Instead I was being reminded how ignorant I am. I turned onto the walk that leads to our front door, noticed our car wasn't in the driveway, realized I must've beaten the parentals home.

"Clive?" I interrupted him.

"What?"

"'Cudgel my brain no more with this.' Okay?"

"Act five," Clive said.

Thanks to my best friend, I now knew I was ignorant about movies, and, worse, I wasn't done with the mystery. Why had Mike chosen our gin joint—our school play, that is? This was a good question.

Clive made a random guess. "Maybe Mike did something bad in life and we're his punishment. You know, like Hamlet's ghost 'doom'd for a certain term to walk the night and for the day confined to fast in fires.'"

"Act one," I said, fumbling for my key, turning the knob. "I don't think we're *that* bad, Clive. And anyway, it doesn't matter."

"How do you figure?" Clive asked.

Inside at last, I juggled backpack, phone, and coat, bumped the door closed with my butt, dropped into the best chair in the living room. "Whyever he's here, the important part is stick to the plan. I tell Emma who Mike is, show her a photo, she stops threatening us with the No-Trauma script, the show goes on. Right?"

"Bring up Humphrey Bogart and Ingrid Bergman if you have to," Clive said.

Now I was exasperated. "What? Why—"

"One more thing, bro."

"Yeah?"

"Way to be! You did it! You saved the show!"

I grinned. Good old Clive.

CHAPTER TWENTY-SEVEN

Since I couldn't talk to Emma about Mike in front of everybody, I had to get her alone, which was way harder than I expected.

For days and days I got up as soon as Mom woke me, asked Obi-Wan for help, and ate breakfast in a hurry—all so I could get to the caf before school and catch Emma.

Only Emma was never there.

Maybe her parents didn't have to get to work so early anymore. Maybe people in Plattsfield had stopped getting divorced and fighting over money.

I couldn't talk to Emma at lunch or after school, either. She was always in a cluster of girls.

Was she avoiding me? Why? Wasn't she afraid of Mike anymore? Meanwhile, no one made us go back to the No-Trauma script, and rehearsals settled into a routine. We did stretching exercises. We checked our props backstage. We spent a few moments getting into character—in my case four characters. And then Mia, the stage manager, announced: "The scene is Elsinore," which, in case you forgot, is the name of the Hamlet family castle in Denmark.

After that, we got to work for real. Mike had put tape on the floor of the stage to show us where stuff would be when we got a set—the walls of the castle, Claudius's and Gertrude's thrones, the headstones and the grave in the graveyard. Once the whole play had been blocked, meaning once Mike and us actors had worked out where we were supposed to enter and exit and move around onstage, we rehearsed over and over, first scene by scene, then act by act.

Besides Justin in the booth—the guy who let there be light, I mean—all us players helped out with crew stuff like pulling the curtains and minding the props, which meant we had more to memorize. It was my job, for example, in act three to listen for a trumpet blast provided by the holy spirit and then hand torches (really broomsticks) to Lila and Brianna to carry when they marched onstage with Clive and Sarah.

If I forgot, Mia hissed at me: "*Noah!*"

Really, she had the hardest job of all. She had to

know what everybody was supposed to be doing at all times and then remind us to actually do it.

Also, she had to manage Diego, which was like a whole job by itself. The kid had a big part—Horatio, Hamlet's best friend. But he seemed to be more interested in snapping photos than in making his entrances and remembering his lines. His idea of hilarious was sneaking up behind Emma and batting her with one of the gift-wrap tubes we used for swords.

TBH, I thought that was kind of funny too, and sometimes even Emma smiled.

After each rehearsal, there was something called notes, when we sat in the house and Mike told us what was good and what wasn't. When I read up on Mike Einstein in life, I found out he'd been tough on actors and had a temper, but he also made a lot of jokes.

The jokes part was still the same.

But the tough part?

Maybe dying chills a person out.

Mike was positive and patient, treated us sixth graders like, yeah, Shakespeare was hard, but we could get the hang of it, we could do a good job, impress our families, impress the whole darned town of Plattsfield.

Since he believed it, so did we.

Of course, I thought of confronting Mike, telling him I knew who he was, who he used to be. But Clive and I talked it over, and we thought: Why? Probably his ghostly knowledge had already picked up the news, besides which, everything was going great. Why risk messing it up?

Likewise, I finally stopped worrying about Emma, gave up on reporting my findings to her. Clive and I had a theory about why she'd gone AWOL: Probably she had realized she'd be the least popular Sixth-Grade Player in the history of Plattsfield-Winklebottom Memorial if she carried out her threat, if she either blabbed to everybody and got Mike in trouble, or made us go back to the No-Trauma *Hamlet*. We had all worked too hard to let anything bad happen to our show. All of us wanted our *Hamlet* to be fabulous.

But Emma couldn't admit she was powerless to get what she wanted. That would be the same as surrender, not part of her personality. Her only option was avoid the issue and avoid me.

It was a good theory. I only wish it had turned out to be true.

CHAPTER TWENTY-EIGHT

Monday, Rehearsal Week Four, 12 Days till Performance

Then came the Monday everything changed.

Clive and I walked to rehearsal that day with Diego and Madeline. Madeline was more chatty than usual, talking about a Broadway show her grandparents took her to one time when she was little.

Clive pushed open the door to the house. Behind him, we all trooped in, looked up, and stopped . . . too awestruck and amazed to move on.

Clive and I and Diego, I mean. Madeline was still talking and kept talking until Clive said: "Holy Hamlet's ghost!" and Diego said, "Heck yeah!" and I said, "Hush up, Madeline—*look*!"

Onstage at the previous rehearsal: dusty floorboards and folding chairs. Onstage now: Elsinore!

Laughing, whooping, not even believing what we saw in front of us—Clive and I ran down the aisle, vaulted onto the stage, sprinted up four steps to the castle rampart, the place where the sentries are standing in scene one when they see the ghost glide past. The steps, the wall, the castle keep—none of it was made of plywood and paint like every other set I'd ever heard of. The whole thing was probably fake. It had to be fake. But it seemed as rough and sturdy as real stone.

Upstage, left of center, a gaping drawbridge formed an arch, behind which was the throne room. More fakery, I bet, but it sure looked like velvet and gold and marble and dark wood. Downstage from that was a courtyard, suitable for a duel or, if you rolled in the headstones on a platform from backstage, a funeral.

Soon all the players had arrived, and, like little kids, we explored. Every few seconds someone exclaimed: "You can, like, raise the drawbridge with this crank!" "Is that real moss on this headstone?" "You guys, I swear, there are fish in the moat!"

Fooling around, Diego discovered that the throne room sat on a turntable, which of course he had to spin real fast, same as the merry-go-round at the old playground.

"Don't do that, Diego. You'll break something!"

Mia warned, and she was right. He would've broken Eddie, only Eddie is a star athlete and jumped into the moat before the far side of the turntable swung around, revealing the chapel where guilty Claudius prays.

"Look at this!" said Sarah, who played Gertrude. "Change out the altar for this chest, and now the chapel's the queen's chamber—*my* chamber! Isn't it just adorable?"

"Not the word I would have used," Clive said.

"Awesome," I said, "is the only possible word."

Behind the scenery was a painted backdrop, and it was awesome, too, not that I'm any kind of art expert. On it the towers and back walls of the castle snaked away into the distance, and hills covered in gray-green forest shimmered beneath a steely sky.

Only Emma was unimpressed—no surprise.

I mean, if Mike's razzle-dazzle tricks had not impressed her, then what would?

I think we were all starting to wonder why Mike was so late when—second shock of the day—Fig came in, headset and all, looking into the great far-away and talking about pineapple. "Hold on," he said to the headset. "Where's Mike got to anyway? I've got a thousand parents who want to know—oh!"

Having departed the land of the headset, he noticed Elsinore at last.

"Looking for me?" Since we were about to rehearse the graveyard scene, the platform with the headstones had been rolled onstage. Now Mike appeared from behind one, rose from the grave, in other words. "Sorry I'm late. One of Gertrude's gowns needed a button, and—"

"Wait, wait, wait," said Sarah. "*Gowns?* Plural?"

"Costumes are in the music room downstairs, the one the girls will be using as a dressing room," Mike said. "Feel free to take a look."

Squealing, a surge of girls departed.

"Fan-*tas*-tic!" said Fig, amazed like the rest of us. "But how did you build it so fast?"

All humble-brag, Mike shrugged. "I did some drawing, made some calls."

"Well, it ought to shut up the parents for a bit," Fig said. "I don't mind saying I've been running interference on your behalf."

Of the girls, only Emma had stuck around onstage. Maybe she wasn't that interested in the costume for Polonius. "What about fake blood?" she wanted to know. "We'll need a lot. *And* swords. Besides which, when do we block the duel between

Laertes and Hamlet? Every time we get to that in the script, Mike says TK—to come."

Coach Fig frowned. "You okay, Miss Jessel? Bad case of stage fright?"

"No!" Emma said. "I just think *someone* ought to be *responsible!*"

"Now, just you hang on a mo," said Fig. "Is that comment directed at me? Because it might interest you to know, Emma Jessel, that—" He went silent, cocked his head, held up a finger, looked into the faraway. "What's that? Never heard of such an allergy. Bride or groom's side?"

Mike looked after him briefly, then clapped his hands. "All right, everyone, back to work. Today we tackle the final scene, and yes, Miss Jessel, this should make you happy. It's time to choreograph the combat."

CHAPTER TWENTY-NINE

When the girls returned from their dressing room, Madeline was again talking about the Broadway show she'd seen with her grandparents. But no one was paying attention, and Mia, clutching her clipboard, consulting her stopwatch, broke in: "All right, people. The scene is *Elsinore!*"

"And how," said Clive.

The end of the real *Hamlet* is exciting, bloody, and sad. Hamlet and his best friend, Laertes (Fuli and Marley), have a sword fight in front of an audience of almost the whole cast.

Spoiler alert: Claudius has dipped one of the swords in poison and, as a result, both Laertes and Hamlet die. Afterward—fanfare, please!—Fortinbras, King of Norway, quite a large country, enters from the wings to do mop-up.

Up till today, Fuli and Marley had hammered each other with cardboard gift-wrap tubes, but along with the set and the costumes, a couple of swords had appeared. Give a kid a weapon and there's bound to be fooling around, even if the kid is a girl. Not to mention every time Fuli or Marley put her sword down, either Diego or Eddie picked it up and ripped at the air and made samurai noises.

Finally, Mike got us settled and asked a question. "What is the number one rule in stage combat?"

Everyone looked at everyone else. Finally, Sarah said, "Don't actually kill anybody?"

"Correct," said Mike.

"*I* think we shouldn't have swords until we know how to use them appropriately," Emma said. "*My* parents—"

"Oh, *your* parents!" said Eddie Muir. "Best day of rehearsal ever and you're trying to mess it up."

Marley chimed in. "Give it a rest, Emma. Please?"

Mia said, "You know, Emma, you are not the boss. Even if you aspire to be."

Emma said, "Oh, because, you *are*, Mia?"

"I want the show to be good," Mia said. "That's what we all want, right?"

"Heck yeah!" said Diego.

Now everyone was glaring at Emma, whose face glowed sunburn red. It must hurt to be ganged up on that way. A good person would feel sympathy. Maybe I'm not so good? Emma had tried to blackmail Mike and sabotage the show. If she was miserable, I was glad. She deserved it.

Mike stepped in. "Miss Jessel has a point," he said. "Theater history is littered with the corpses of actors slain in mismanaged stage combat."

"I knew it!" said Brianna.

"Totally untrue," Madeline said.

"Then let's not start a trend," Mike said. "Miss Jessel? Where are you going?"

Emma had turned away from us and stomped downstage. She put a hand down to support herself, dropped clunkily to the floor of the house, kept on walking up the aisle.

Mia said, "She can't leave rehearsal. It's not allowed."

Fuli said, "I can go get her."

Mike said, "She just needs a moment. As for the rest of us—Fuli? Marley? It's your duel in act five. Let's get to it. Does anyone else want to give combat a try?"

Everyone did—even Brianna.

"Beyond survival, the priority is learning how to

fall," Mike said. "Falls come in three flavors: side, front, and back. Coach Newton has stacked some mats for us backstage, I think. Let's grab a few, move downstage, and practice."

When it comes to falling, Mike explained, 'tis better to crumple than to keel. That is, go slow, using either knees, hips, or butt to break the impact. Soon the Plattsfield-Winklebottom Memorial Sixth-Grade Players were dropping dead all over the place, which is hard to do without laughing.

"Very good," said Mike. "Tomorrow we'll work on the same thing, only more quietly, please. As for the duel itself, you need three words of vocabulary: lunge, parry, thrust. Then think of it as a dance step. To start, I'll be Hamlet. Laertes—Miss Jacobs? Your place is across from me, here. If you like, the rest of you can pair up and follow along."

"It would be a whole lot better if we each had our own weapons," Eddie grumbled. He didn't mean for Mike to hear, I don't think, but one thing about a ghost, he doesn't have to hear.

"Of course, it would be better, Mr. Muir," Mike agreed. "And luckily, I thought ahead. If one of you could go backstage"—Eddie was on his way—"and look around, I believe you'll find an umbrella stand chock-full of swords, rapiers, and daggers."

Brianna squealed, but Mike reassured her, "Not to worry. The blades are foam core and foil—lightweight, flexible, and harmless."

Eddie's grin was huge as he brought in the umbrella stand and let us choose. I took a shiny Viking sword with a black handle—hilt, I guess it's called—as long as my legs (or Clive's arms) and almost weightless.

Lunge! Parry! Thrust! Mike demoed the swordfight tango; we copied him, or tried to, and—before anyone was ready—the clock read 5:30, another rehearsal done.

CHAPTER THIRTY

Clive's mom was giving me a ride home, so Clive and I walked out together. I was trying to remember the steps to the tango Mike had taught us, the best grip for a dagger, the difference between a rapier and a foil.

I was wondering if there was anything at home for predinner snack.

I wasn't thinking of Emma.

I guess Emma had been thinking of me, though.

Heading down the aud steps, I heard a whispered "*Noah!*" and looked around.

No one there.

"Did you—" I started to ask Clive, but he nodded toward the shrubs to our right, and there, among them, was Emma.

"Are you seriously hiding in the bushes?" I asked.

"No, that is . . . *no*. I'm just here hanging out, uh . . . waiting for *you*."

Shoot, I thought. *Shoulda known. She'd been embarrassed in front of everyone. She'd never leave that alone.*

Clive looked at me. "Do you need backup?"

Yeah, I needed backup. The girl was trouble!

But Emma said, "It's *private*, Clive," and Clive said, "I'll tell my mom to wait," and before I could stop him, he walked off.

"Okay, what?" I asked, sounding tougher than I felt.

The sun was still bright, but there was a chill in the air, and Emma looked like she was cold. "We had a deal," she said. "Who is Mike? Did you find out the way you promised?"

"Yeah, eons ago, but what does it matter now? The performance is next week. No way we're going back to the other script."

"We'll see," Emma said. "Who was he anyway—or who does he *think* he was? And I will expect proof."

No one likes to be ordered around. I wished I could say take a hike. But my brain told me to get this over with. I slipped off my backpack, unzipped the outer pocket, and removed a beat-up piece of paper I'd been carrying for a while—a copy of a profile of Mike Einstein I'd found in a magazine. It had a photo, too.

Emma read it quickly and looked up.

"Never heard of 'im," she said.

"You've heard of Broadway, maybe? You see, he was a big-deal director, not some guy locked up for eating sixth graders. We are way lucky he's even here, Emma, so how 'bout this? You keep your side of the deal: Stay quiet about the ghost stuff. The show goes on and you don't become a . . . whatzitcalled—*pariah!*"

Don't ask me where that word came from. Child of two professors, I guess. It means the ultimate outsider—someone no one will talk to.

Unfortunately, Emma seemed to know the word too. She turned the sunburn shade again. Embarrassed? Hurt? Plain old mad?

I didn't know and only cared because of what she might do.

"I see the resemblance," she said, "but he's not the Mike Einstein in this article. He just thinks he is."

There was no good way to end this conversation. Besides, my stomach was growling.

"Arguing is a waste of time," I said. "You're gonna do what you're gonna do. But if you wreck the show— so help me . . ."

"So help you, *what?*" Emma glared.

So help me, I had no idea. But theater is about making it look good, putting emotion across, digging in and inhabiting the character. By now I could do that.

"Slash! Thrust! Parry!" I did the sword-fight tango. "I know a thing or two about combat, Emma. Just keep that in mind."

CHAPTER THIRTY-ONE

(SCENE: Dining room, early evening. NOAH and DAD are eating takeout Chinese food for dinner.)

NOAH *(looking at his mom's usual place)*: Where's Mom again?

DAD: Department dinner. Those English professors will yak for hours.

NOAH: Physics professors don't yak?

DAD: We write equations on the whiteboard.

NOAH *(skeptical)*: Seriously?

DAD: No. We yak too. How was rehearsal today?

NOAH: It was cool. We have a set now. It's awesome.

DAD: That's good news. I'm looking forward to seeing it. Performance is coming right up, isn't it?

NOAH *(doesn't look up, serves himself from takeout carton)*: Unh-hunh.

DAD: Noah, uh . . . you seem a little, I don't know,

distracted. Are you still disappointed you're not playing Hamlet?

NOAH: Who says I was ever disappointed?

(DAD looks at NOAH, raises eyebrows—were you?)

NOAH *(one-shoulder shrug)*: Maybe a little. *(He recovers.)* But, Dad, I not only play Fortinbras and Gravedigger One, but I *also* play Rosencrantz.

DAD: Slimy character, that guy, along with his good pal Guildenstern.

NOAH *(nods)*: That's what Mike says.

DAD *(takes bite, chews)*: Oh yes?

NOAH: The two of them used to be Hamlet's friends, but now they're secretly working for the bad guy, Claudius.

DAD: Your Mike's insightful, I think. I've always believed you can read Hamlet as a warning to young people: Beware of the old! They don't want to hand over power. They do sneaky, wretched things to keep it.

NOAH *(nods)*: Mike says that, too, which is why there's so much spying. Old Polonius is the worst. He spies on his own children. He spies on Hamlet.

DAD *(stops eating, looks at NOAH, blinks)*: Your Mike says that?

NOAH: My Mike? *(He grins at DAD.)* Sure, okay. My

Mike. But how come you look like the old lady who swallowed a fly?

DAD *(recovers, smiles, shakes head)*: Because most people when they talk about that play, they talk about memory or revenge. Up till now, I only knew one other person who saw the old-versus-young angle.

NOAH *(mouth full, more interested in last bites of stir-fry than literary theory)*: Oh yeah? Who?

DAD *(picks up water glass, drinks, wipes lips, resets, spears bite with fork)*: Nobody that important. Besides, he's long gone.

CHAPTER THIRTY-TWO

Friday, Rehearsal Week Five, 7 Days till Performance

Miss Magnus went to New York City over spring break to see shows and was crossing Broadway, not even jaywalking, when a taxi hit her and broke her leg in three places, and that's how it started.

Remember?

If it seems long ago, I'm with you, but the point is that one apparently random, unconnected thing, such as that taxi, can trigger a cascade of bloody and unnatural acts, accidental judgments, and casual slaughters. (Act five.)

And that's exactly how it worked—more or less—when Mr. Garrier, my math teacher, delayed my arrival at rehearsal.

If you've wondered how I, an average sixth grader, could possibly keep up with all the demands of *Hamlet,* as well as Nate-the-Great detecting, preventing Emma from blabbing about Mike, and snacks, and homework, the answer is I didn't.

And guess what suffered?

If you said snacks, you have never met a sixth-grade boy.

The right answer is homework, *duh,* and after school that day Mr. Garrier asked me—already on my feet and moving fast toward the door—to stay back one minute for a chat.

"I have rehearsal," I said, still in motion.

"Do the words 'summer school' mean anything to you?" he asked.

I stopped, turned around, faced Mr. Garrier.

"Glad to have your attention," he said. "Your math grade is in free fall. What are you going to do about it?"

"Try harder?" I suggested.

"Look, I realize you're busy. I'm looking forward to the play myself. Still, I doubt you want to spend your summer in math class."

"Summer is sacred," I said.

"My sentiments too, and so I have a proposal." Mr. Garrier nodded at some papers on the corner of his desk. "Here lie a few extra-credit worksheets to complete by Monday."

He picked up the worksheets, handed them over. I swear there were a hundred. How could I possibly find time to do them this weekend—Hell Weekend, when the Plattsfield-Winklebottom Memorial Sixth-Grade Players would be at rehearsal day and night?

And speaking of rehearsal, I had to get going. We were working on the graveyard scene that day. Grave-digger One (me!) was kind of important.

If I was late, Mike would be annoyed and Mia would kill me.

"No problem, Mr. Garrier," I lied, heading for the door. "Thanks a lot. See you Monday."

Down the hallway, out the door, across the court-yard, up the steps—I ran to the aud in record time, expecting Mike to be frowning and Mia to be yell-ing, which in the end would have been preferable because what I actually saw was this: Emma onstage about to deliver a special recitation.

"I *expect* you're wondering *why* I have called you *here* today—" Emma said.

"No one's wondering. It's rehearsal. Get to the point." That was Mia, in case you had any doubt. She was onstage trading lethal looks with Emma. Every-one else was sitting in the first two rows of the house.

The interruption gave me my chance. Create a

distraction! Go big or go home! Keep Emma from wrecking the show!

It was up to me, Noah McNichol.

"Hello! Hello! Hello! Sorry I'm late. What did I miss? Yorick still dead?"

It was boffo, if I do say so myself.

Only Emma wasn't impressed. "It won't work, Noah." She turned her lethal look on me.

"Oh yes? What about this?" Someone had left a sword among the headstones. I gripped it, brandished it, cried: "En garde!"

Up in the booth, the holy spirit was watching because—*bzzzzz*—he let there be light, specifically a spotlight on me, Noah McNichol. Emma stepped back, and the audience gasped. For a moment I waved my sword, my triumph in sight.

Then Emma parried with an age-old trick.

She rolled her eyes.

And, like that, my spotlight dimmed. "Your sword's not real, Noah," she said. "None of this is real. *Not* the headstones, *not* the chapel, not *Elsinore*. And as for your *director—*"

"Don't say it!" Clive called from his seat in the house.

"He's as *fake* as everything else," Emma said. "He *claims* he's a ghost, and he's *not*."

Brianna squealed. "A *ghost?*"

"Cool!" said Eddie Muir.

"Heck yeah!" said Diego, and after that there were lots of comments, and soon the aud got noisy.

"Besides that"— Emma raised her voice to be heard —"Noah and Clive know all about it, and they're so *dumb*, they believe him."

"Clive and I are not the dumb ones," I said, wishing I still had my spotlight, "just by the way. And maybe you've forgotten, but you and I had a deal, which makes you a dirty, low-down, thieving double-crosser."

This line was not from *Hamlet*. I think maybe I borrowed it from another classic, *SpongeBob SquarePants*.

"Just wait till I tell my *parents*," Emma said, and then, even without the help of the holy spirit, I thought I saw some light.

"You haven't told them yet?" I said.

"Mike has one more chance to give in to my demand." Emma had crossed her arms over her chest.

"Demand?" From behind a headstone came a voice, disembodied at first. But then Mike himself appeared, and he looked the same as usual, his too too solid flesh in no danger either of melting or resolving into dew. (Act one.)

"She wants to go back to the old script, the No-Trauma script," I explained.

"No, I don't. Not anymore. My demand is different now because, uh . . . something happened," Emma said.

What was she talking about?

"I think I know what she means," Mia said, and, ever helpful, she held up her phone so we could all see.

"No, wait. Don't show them!" Emma said. "Don't look, everybody!"

Everybody looked. The mysterious D. Avventura had made another masterpiece, #EmmaIsPolonius, thirteen seconds in which still photos of regular Emma—at lunch, in class, in the hallway—morphed into the character of Polonius. The first images showed Emma herself at rehearsal, then there was a series of what must've been actors who played him in the movies, even Zazu, the bird in *The Lion King*. The end was a clip of Emma falling down dead, *thud*, and behind it the sound of slow clapping.

Technically, it was good, I guess. And it was funny too—clever. Still, I wasn't sure how I would've felt if it had been about me.

"Oh, come on, Emma," said Sarah. "It's not like

we haven't seen it a thousand times already. It's a D. Avventura classic!"

"You've all seen it?" Emma said weakly.

"Not me," I said, and then, because Emma looked like she might stumble, I grabbed her elbow. "Here. Sit in Gertrude's chair. And, uh . . . take deep breaths or whatever."

"So, Emma—Miss Jessel. What is your demand?" Mike asked, and—even though she'd been threatening him two seconds ago—his voice was kind.

Emma looked around desperately, like what she wanted now was escape.

Then she shocked us all.

"I want to play Ophelia! I want to be young and glamorous and crazy, not a pompous old man." She looked at Madeline. "*Please!* Just this one tiny favor and I'll never ask you for anything again for the rest of my life? *I swear!*"

It was like watching tennis or something. Everybody had been looking at Emma, and now we turned to Madeline, whose face showed confusion then concern. This lasted about a nanosecond. "No, Emma. Just no."

Of course, Emma could never play Ophelia, not even if Madeline had said okay. It was too late for such a big change. Still, even I had to feel bad for Emma. She was so upset.

After that, it was Mike who did something surprising.

He turned to Diego, gave him a stern look. "Mr. Arcati? Do you have anything you'd like to tell us?"

Diego adjusted his beret, which that day was tan with a plaid pattern. "Heck no," he said, but without the usual energy. "I mean, it wasn't me."

And the way he said it, you could tell it meant exactly the opposite. Diego had made the PicPoc.

Mike raised his eyebrows.

Then he raised Diego. That is, he—Mike—tilted his face upward, and as he did, Diego rose as well— one foot, two feet, three feet into the air. On cue, the holy spirit gave him a spotlight, too.

"Hey! No!" cried Diego. Motionless at first, he was flailing now. His beret slipped sideways and dropped to the stage, then his round glasses. "Put me down! OMG, you really are a ghost!"

Brianna—skittish, easily freaked-out Brianna— put it together before anybody else: "Diego is D. Avventura!"

"Of course!" said somebody, and, "That kid? No way!" and, "Shoulda known!"

"Okay, okay, I made the PicPoc," Diego cried. "But I didn't mean to be mean or anything. It was more of an . . . an *homage*."

A what?

Mike grinned, tried to stifle it, failed. "Oh, is that what it was? Did you perhaps think about how Ms. Jessel would receive it?"

"I thought she'd be flattered? Can I come down now?"

CHAPTER THIRTY-THREE

Mike nodded. Diego dropped.

"In the future, think before you post, Mr. Arcati," Mike said. "From now on, if you don't, someone just might be watching . . . from beyond the grave."

A far-off organ played a minor chord, the footlights flickered like candles, bat shadows flitted among the clouds above, thunder boomed. Was the holy ghost in the booth fooling around?

Or was Mike?

Either way, the Plattsfield-Winklebottom Memorial Sixth-Grade Players stood in silence, stunned, their hearts—like mine—pounding.

Then Eddie Muir turned on Emma, palms upraised. "Are you crazy? Being directed by a ghost is the best thing *ever!*"

Emma replied, "There's no such thing as ghosts," but her voice was meek.

"So," Mike asked, all business, "are we good here? Any questions?"

"What the heck is *homage*?" Clive asked.

Now Mike grinned for real. "A tribute?"

Clive nodded and translated. "Props," he said.

For a few moments, the silence persisted, and I don't mind telling you I felt dizzy. Mike was a ghost, everybody knew it, Emma didn't want the old script, she wanted to play Ophelia, Diego, aka D. Avventura, had been levitated before our eyes . . . and now we were just going to rehearse like normal?

Yes, except . . .

There would be one more surprise in the graveyard that afternoon.

"No time for questions." Mia waved the clipboard. "Places, everybody. Brianna? Noah? This is act five. The scene is Elsinore, a graveyard."

By this time it was reflex to follow Mia's orders. Fuli grabbed Yorick's skull and a spade from the prop table while Marley and I dragged Ophelia's coffin onstage so that Madeline could lie down and get comfy.

In this scene, Brianna and I are digging a grave

for poor Ophelia who has drowned. Hamlet and Horatio are—guess what?—spying on them, not knowing whose grave it is. Later, Gertrude, Claudius, and Laertes will show up for the funeral.

Brianna and I picked up our spades and took our places on the platform beside the coffin. The platform was raised off the stage, and beneath it was just enough room for a shallow built-in grave. In the hole was a pile of dirt, something to shovel.

"How are you feeling today, Gravedigger One?" Mike asked me.

"Just another workday," I said, in character. "I don't care much who I'm burying."

"Miss Larkin? Gravedigger Two? How about you?"

"The whole thing gives me the shivers," Brianna said.

"Gives *you* the shivers, or your character?" Mike asked.

"Me!"

"Do you think the audience will get the shivers?" Mike asked.

Brianna grinned. "I hope so," she said, then she thought a second. "Only maybe not at the beginning of the scene? Because Noah's character, he makes jokes. It's like he thinks death is funny."

"Maybe he makes jokes to keep his mind off his work, to keep from getting depressed," I said.

Mike nodded. "Excellent thinking. Both of you. Most of the time, this scene is played for laughs. After all, it's the last chance the audience gets to smile before the tragedy becomes unbearable. How about if we try it that way, keep it light, see how we do?"

Gravedigger One had the first line: "'Is she to be buried in Christian burial?'"

The idea was if Ophelia killed herself, that's a sin, and back then she wouldn't have been allowed to have the same service Christians usually get.

I forgot about Emma. I forgot about Mike. I forgot I was only a Plattsfield-Winklebottom Memorial Sixth-Grade Player, that Madeline's eyes were open, that her padded casket looked pretty comfortable. I opened my mouth to speak and . . .

. . . Madeline sat up, scaring me half to death. I mean, a ghost for a director? Fine. Used to it. But this was too much. Ophelia's corpse was not supposed to sit up in her coffin.

"I have a question." Madeline looked at Mike, who was by now seated in the first row of the house.

"No, you don't!" Mia said from the wings. "You're dead!"

"Never stopped me," Mike said.

"I saw a show you directed once when I was little. There were stars in it, movie stars. Back in your time, what was it like to work with them?" Madeline asked.

Mike did not seem surprised by the question. "'My time' indeed!" he said. "It wasn't that long ago, and, for the most part, it was a pleasure. A few of the big names were egotists, of course, believed their own press clippings, wouldn't take direction, but many more—"

"Wait, wait, wait a minute." In the wings, sensible Marley awaited her entrance as Laertes. "What are you talking about? Our very own ghost directed movie stars? For reals?"

Brianna, naturally, shrieked.

Mia tossed her clipboard in the air. "I give up."

I looked down at Madeline, leaned on my spade. "So you know who he is."

"He's Mike Einstein," Madeline said. "Didn't everybody know?"

"Never heard of 'im," Sarah said.

"I thought he looked familiar," Diego said.

"Liar," Eddie said.

Madeline shook her head. "Some drama geeks you are. The man's a legend."

"I wouldn't go that far," Mike said. "Mythic maybe."

Clive looked at Madeline. "So you knew all along. But did you know he was a ghost?"

"Well," Madeline said. "I knew Mike Einstein died in 2014. So ghost seemed the most likely explanation. I mean, 'there are more things in heaven and earth . . .'"

CHAPTER THIRTY-FOUR

Sunday, Rehearsal Week Six, 5 Days till Performance:

In the end, Emma's blackmail scheme failed spectacularly. We didn't go back to the No-Trauma script. She didn't get to play Ophelia. The show went on.

How come?

Shakespeare had an explanation. It was right there in *Hamlet,* act four, the part where Claudius decides he can't kill Hamlet the way he wants to because Hamlet is so popular with all the Danish people. "Loved of the distracted multitude" is how he says it. If Claudius had killed Hamlet, or locked him up, the people would have rebelled.

Same deal with the Sixth-Grade Players. Mike was popular. Anything anyone did to get rid of him—we would have rebelled too.

I still didn't get why Emma had caused all this drama in the first place, or why Diego had made that

PicPoc. If I had a chance, I would ask Clive. All those seasons of *Gossip Girl* later, he understood human nature better than I did.

Meanwhile, I was way too busy to worry about any of it. The Plattsfield-Winklebottom Memorial Sixth-Grade Players rehearsed all weekend, according to the schedule, with Emma playing the prating knave Polonius and Madeline the glamorous, tortured Ophelia.

Justin, the holy ghost in the booth, turned out to be a tech wizard. With his help, we got the lights and sound operating smoothly, even the cordless mics—lavaliers, they're called—that were clipped to our costumes. At first they squealed, they rasped, they hummed, defying adjustment both human and supernatural until, at last, they were working fine.

We didn't see Coach Fig all weekend, till late Sunday afternoon when he showed up like a hero with sodas and two trays of dumplings from Himalaya.

We greeted him with a standing O.

"Thank you, thank you, thank you very much." Fig raised a hand to acknowledge the crowd. "I'm just happy to be here."

The dumplings were gone in five minutes. After

that, we licked grease from our fingers and finished off the sodas.

Fig was wearing his headset, of course, but for once he was among us, having returned to planet Earth from the faraway realm of the wedding planner.

"You've spent a great deal of time on one wedding, Coach," Mike said.

"Couple o' rich kids and, worse yet, their rich parents," Coach Fig said.

"When does the wedding take place?" Mike asked.

"Next Saturday, two in the afternoon, reception to follow at five," Fig said. "For directions and details, see the website."

Mike grinned. "You'll be relieved when it's over."

"Won't I, though," Fig agreed. "And speaking of upcoming events, I've been meaning to ask, how go ticket sales for the performance? It's coming up on Friday, correct-o?"

"Ticket sales?" Mike repeated. "Am I in charge of ticket sales?"

"Uh . . . well, sure. Someone has to do it," Fig said. "I haven't had much time, and . . ." He shrugged.

Mike nodded thoughtfully. "I see. The thing is, though, I don't know much about selling tickets.

I've never been asked to oversee the business side of things."

Clive looked at me. "Uh-oh."

Emma piled on. "He hasn't gotten the blood, either."

Coach Fig made a face. "Blood?"

"For Polonius? For Hamlet and Laertes? *How* are we supposed to *die* without any blood?" Emma said.

I had been afraid of this. Emma had been on her best behavior all weekend, but now her native orneriness came out.

"Oh dear, I do keep forgetting the blood," Mike said. "Perhaps I've grown squeamish in my dotage. Anyone have any ideas?"

To everyone's surprise, it was Brianna who spoke up—anxious Brianna who hates all things gory or sad. "I'll take care of it. I have an idea."

Did she? I wondered. Or was she like the rest of us, tired of Emma's drama?

Either way, Emma gave her a dirty look, and Brianna responded, sweet as pie: "Would you like to help me, Emma?"

"No," Emma said.

Everyone looked at her.

"Oh, fine, I'll help," Emma said.

"Good woman," Mike said. "And as for ticket sales?"

"I'll do it," Mia said. "I have an idea too."

I don't know if you've ever tried to do a million math worksheets after two solid days of rehearsal, half a dozen Himalaya dumplings (both veggie and meat), and two full cans of soda.

If not, you're missing out.

I bet if you're my smart dad, the physics professor, you think math is as much fun as *ShredSauce.* Relaxing, even. You would have looked forward to those worksheets at the same time you chowed down on dumplings.

Unfortunately, I am not my smart dad.

Also, I'm not much of an actor, I guess. Not as good as Fuli at least. In fact, so far as I can tell, I have no particular talent at all.

I wouldn't even make it as an apple picker because, according to Clive, the two things you need to make it as an apple picker are long arms and quickness.

I lack both.

But maybe I do have one talent, if you want to call it a talent. Maybe I've always had it, but I didn't notice till now—till I didn't get cast as Hamlet, I mean, till I survived that and moved on.

What is that talent? I can make the best of things, like playing Marcellus, Rosencrantz, Gravedigger One, and Fortinbras. And one day, maybe, if I paid attention to the way Fuli inhabited the character, the way Madeline became sad, crazy Ophelia, even the way Clive dug deep and found his inner villain— maybe one day I'd get a bigger part.

When I got the chance, I'd ask Mike about that. And I'd ask him a hundred other questions, too, like how is it in the afterlife, really? Are the Jews right or the Christians or the Muslims or who?

Then there was the gin-joint question. What's a formerly famous Broadway director, now a five-star ghost, doing in Plattsfield, New York?

But all that was for later. Right now, Sunday night, I was a person failing math and facing the horror of summer school.

"Help me, Obi-Wan," I said to the poster on my wall.

And then I sharpened a pencil and leaned back against the pillows on my bed, notebook on my knees, and slogged through worksheets one by one.

CHAPTER THIRTY-FIVE

Monday, Rehearsal Week Six, 4 Days till Performance

Finally, we had a nice warm day, and the school opened the caf so, if we wanted, we could sit under the shelter outside at the old picnic tables and benches. They are made of wood. Having soaked up the damp all winter, they felt sticky, but we didn't care. It was glorious to be in clean air with the smell of clean air, instead of cooked vegetables, wet wool, and the skin of fellow humans.

That day the caf rotation delivered hot dogs, either regular meat or the fake kind. By the time you're a sixth grader, you know that, with mustard, they taste totally the same.

Fuli, Clive, and I sat down. Madeline came out with her tray. I waved her over. I didn't bother to get permission. I knew it would be okay.

Madeline was talking before she got halfway to

our table. "You were awesome at rehearsal yesterday."

"Hey, thanks," I said. "Which part did you like
best? In my humble opinion, I really shine when
I'm Rosencrantz and I say, 'My lord, you must tell us
where the body is.'"

"Not you, Noah," Madeline said, settling in. "Fuli.
When you say that part in the soliloquy, that part
about the undiscovered country? You make me see it
in my head, like I'm on a boat at night, heading for
rocks a long way away."

"That's just Vermont," I said.

"Funny guy," Clive said.

"Thank you, Madeline," Fuli said. "Do you want
to know something? Hamlet means death is like a
visit to the undiscovered country. But when I say it,
I'm thinking of Plattsfield. When my family moved
here—to us, that's what it was."

I shrugged, sipped my milk. "Plattsfield? Death?
Same difference, right?"

Clive was next to me and shoved me. "Is everything funny to you, dude?"

I believe I mentioned already that Clive is my best
friend. And now he'd made me feel stupid. Again.

He's good at that. I took a bite of my dog, wiped mustard off my lips, listened to the awkward quiet. Then I had a thought. "The thing with Emma wasn't funny," I said. "I really thought she might get Mike in trouble, wreck the show. I didn't want that to happen. What is with her, anyway?"

I had chewed another bite before I noticed it was quiet. I looked up. Was I imagining things? Or were Fuli, Madeline, and Clive trading looks? "Okay, what?" I said.

"Earth to Noah," Clive said. "Seriously?"

"I thought you knew," Madeline said, which was pretty funny coming from Madeline, who, till lately, I considered queen of the airheads.

"Even I know," Fuli said.

"I cannot believe this," I said. "I cannot believe *you*. Will somebody please—"

"She likes you, Noah," Clive said. "Emma does. That's why she always sits next to you. That's why she smiles like Christmas when you're around."

"Like Hanukkah, you mean," I said.

"It's kind of sweet, actually," Madeline said.

"No! It is not sweet!" I said.

"And do you want to know what else?" Fuli

asked. "Diego likes *her*. And sometimes when you like somebody, you seek their attention."

"Even their bad attention," Clive said.

"It is just as it is in the play," Fuli went on. "When Hamlet is so mean to Ophelia? He loves her. But his life is falling apart, and he is afraid to show it. He treats her badly, and that's why."

"What Hamlet did to Ophelia was abusive, Gillian says," said Clive. "And Diego should learn better ways to show he likes someone."

I ate the last bite of hot dog, drank the last gulp of milk, looked around for the cookie that was supposed to be dessert, then remembered I'd eaten it before I sat down. Finally, I had a thought. "Maybe if Shakespeare were alive today, he'd be making PicPocs like D. Avventura."

"Good one, dude!" Clive said. "You're comparing Diego to Shakespeare?"

Fuli backed me up. "The art teacher, Ms. Mock, she believes Diego is a genius. I thought it was only because she likes those hats he wears, those round glasses, but perhaps she is correct."

I shook my head. "Want to know something funny? I started sitting with you so I could avoid episodes of *Lunchtime Drama*."

"Brought to you today by the caf's world-famous hot dogs!" Clive said.

"You cannot avoid the lunchtime drama," Fuli said. "It is fundamental."

Clive nodded. "The girl knows whereof she speaks," he said. "And because of that, you should come over to my house sometime, catch some *Gossip Girl* with Gillian and me. You'd definitely learn a lot."

CHAPTER THIRTY-SIX

C live was always telling me I should go over to his house sometime, catch some *Gossip Girl,* get educated about human behavior.

Was he right? Or was I better off the way I'd always been—ignorant?

After lunch, when I should've been paying attention to a PowerPoint about Japanese temples, I thought about the play. In spite of all the spying, Polonius was probably the most ignorant character. He didn't get it about Ophelia and Hamlet, or about Claudius being evil either.

And what happens to Polonius? He loses his daughter and his life.

So maybe there was a moral to *Hamlet*—to that part of it at least.

And maybe, knowing *Hamlet,* I could skip *Gossip Girl.*

Last period that same day, Monday, I turned my math sheets in, expecting a standing O (at least!) from Mr. Garrier. What I got was thumbs-up and a question: "Can you help me get tickets for the show, Noah? Do you have the inside track? I need four."

"Aren't there loads of tickets? The auditorium is huge."

Mr. Garrier shook his head. "Maybe in previous years, but not now, not this year, not when the director of the show is a *ghost*!"

I was speechless, which, you will have noticed, doesn't happen often. "W-w-wait. Wh-who told you that?"

"Common knowledge in the faculty lounge," said Mr. Garrier.

I stalled for time. "And you believe everything you hear in the faculty lounge?"

"Look, Noah." Mr. Garrier got serious. "It doesn't really matter if this ghost thing is mathematically provable. What matters is the story, and given the story, no self-respecting teacher would dare let their family miss out."

I could not argue with Mr. Garrier's logic, if "logic" is the right word, and I said I'd do what I could and then, one more time with feeling, I hotfooted it to the aud, where I found, in the lobby, a long line of people waiting for the box office to open.

"No way!" I said. "All of you are in line for tickets? Tickets to *Hamlet*? The show featuring *me*, Noah McNichol, as Fortinbras, King of Norway?"

A fifth grader who lives on my street said he'd never heard of Norway, but his mom had told him to get in line. Someone else asked if it was true about the ghost and when was the box office supposed to open? She didn't have all day.

"Ghost?" I said. "Ha ha ha—ridiculous. There is no such thing."

A parent who makes sandwiches at Sal's winked and nodded. "I knew it, and there's the proof. Why bother to deny it if it isn't true?"

I opened my mouth but had no answer. "Let me find out about the box office," I said, and went inside to look for Mia, who I finally found down in the dressing room rehanging the costumes.

"Are you some kind of ticket-selling genius, or what?" I asked.

All fake modest, Mia said, "Oh, did that work?"

Mia's idea had been what's called a whisper campaign. First, she told her BFF (best frenemy forever), Nick Frank, that Mike, director of the Plattsfield-

Winklebottom Memorial Sixth-Grade Players' production of *Hamlet* just might maybe be a ghost.

Of course, Nick Frank said, "Yeah, right," so she
told him about floating Diego and the mysterious
flickering footlights and the bats and the switched
scripts and the mind reading and how Mike was a
famous Broadway director, and the famous Broadway
director was dead.

"But, Nick," she continued. "You absolutely cannot tell anybody. This is just between us. I mean,
probably it isn't even true. How could it possibly be
true?"

Nick swore absolutely he would not tell anybody.

And he didn't. Instead, he texted—first his
friend Jen, who texted Clare, who texted Jason,
who is one of those good kids who tells his parents
stuff, so he did tell his parents, and within hours,
it was all over Plattsfield-Winklebottom Memorial,
even in the faculty lounge, how this movie star had
come back from the dead to direct *Hamlet,* or possibly *Hamilton,* and the performance was Friday
night, and it was going to be awesome and supernatural—*live bats!*—and you'd better get tickets
now or miss out.

Mia said she'd save tickets for Mr. Garrier in the

interest of my math grade; then she told me what to tell the people waiting.

Back in the lobby, the line snaked out the door. "Box office opens at three forty-five," I recited. "Tickets are five dollars each, four-ticket limit. Festival seating. One performance only, this Friday at seven. Be there if you dare!"

All during rehearsal, Mia sent runners out to the lobby to keep us players updated. "Seventy-five tickets sold!" was the first report. Then 150, then 310, and after that the reports became a countdown of seats remaining: Ninety-nine! Sixty! Ten!

And finally, after only one hour and forty-seven minutes, the Plattsfield-Winklebottom Memorial Sixth-Grade Play had sold out for the first time in recorded history!

Who deserved credit?

Mia for her marketing?

Mike for being a ghost?

Mike's opinion was neither, at least not entirely. "*Hamlet* is a beloved classic," he told us. "You kids are a top-notch cast. Naturally, the theatergoing public has responded."

On Tuesday, Brianna brought the blood.

The no-budget alternative blood, that is—a trash bag half-filled with plastic packets of ketchup, which Brianna, Emma, and her friends had sneaked one by one from tables in the caf and, when those ran out, from the burger places of Plattsfield.

"Clever," Mike said, regarding the heap of ketchup packets Brianna had dumped onstage. "Potentially very messy, but clever. Mr. Arcati?" Mike looked around, caught Diego's eye.

"I won't go near 'em, I swear," Diego said.

"See that you don't, Horatio," Mike said. "In point of fact, you are one of the few characters that survives the play unbloodied."

"Heck yeah!" said Diego.

His beret was orange that day, and I guess he'd recovered from the whole levitation thing because he seemed as energetic as normal.

Clive said, "If Mrs. Winklebottom had a friend in the caf, she'd know now we ditched that No-Trauma stuff."

Marley said, "That is bats, Clive. Stage blood isn't the *only* explanation for disappearing ketchup."

Clive said, "Oh yeah? Name another one."

Marley said, "I'm thinking."

Mike said, "I think it unlikely the dear lady has

a cafeteria friend. Has anyone heard any concerns from her recently? I haven't even seen Coach Fig since Sunday."

None of us had, and Fuli said, "I guess that means we're out here on our own."

Right on cue, the minor-key organ chord sounded, and there followed the usual shebang: lightning, bat shadows, flickering haunted candles.

Justin, the holy spirit in the booth, typically played games on his phone unless we were actually rehearsing. That day, though, he must've been paying attention.

CHAPTER THIRTY-SEVEN

Thursday, Final Dress Rehearsal, 1 Day till Performance

The sun went away. The clouds came back. By Thursday, the May weather was typical and unlovely in Plattsfield, the sky solid gray, the air—as Shakespeare might have said—nipping and eager. (Act one.)

Seated in the first two rows of the house, we Sixth-Grade Players barely knew and didn't care. We'd been living in the aud so long that we might as well have been mushrooms, oblivious to the wide world beyond.

Mike was upstage right, pacing along the ramparts of Elsinore. Mia was downstage left, beside the open drawbridge, consulting her clipboard.

"Now, don't you worry if today's full dress is a full-dress mess," Mike told us. "A thousand and one things will probably go wrong. Never mind! Keep going!

Think of errors as good luck. The worst run-throughs often precede the best performances! Mr. Arcati?"

"Heck yeah!" Diego said.

"Heck yeah is right!" Mike said. "Miss Duffy?"

"Curtain goes up at four," Mia said. "That gives you twenty-five minutes for costumes and makeup. Starting *now*, everybody. Let's do this thing."

We got to our feet, shuffled toward the stairs that led down to the changing rooms, but before we reached them—*thump-squeal*—the door to the house swung upon, and Coach Fig came jogging toward us down the aisle.

Right away we could tell that something was wrong.

I mean, he wasn't wearing his headset.

In one bound, the coach jumped onstage, pivoted to face us. There was a moment of silence, a Sixth-Grade Player intake of breath.

Had Mrs. Winklebottom found out about the script? Had some parent decided a ghost was an inappropriate director?

Was he here to cancel the show?

Coach Fig spoke: "The wedding is off!"

Madeline asked, "What wedding?"

Mike looked pained for real. "Oh, Coach, I'm so sorry. What happened? Was it the pineapple?"

"It was. The groom's aunt breaks all out in hives if she's even in a room with the stuff, the bride's mother said you have to have it or it's not fruit salad, and the groom accused the bride of trying to poison half his family, and then"—Fig shook his head, reliving the bad memory—"things got ugly."

"How very Shakespearean," said Mike.

Fig shrugged. "I wouldn't know about that. What I do know is I've spent months of my life planning this wedding, and now I've got surplus food, surplus flowers, a surplus DJ, and surplus cake coming my way on Saturday."

Mike removed the green-glowing tablet thingy from his pocket. "I'll drop you a text, Coach. Could be I have an idea to help with that."

Even though Fig was nodding, I don't think he heard. "If you'll excuse me," he said, "I have some calls to make," and, as efficiently as he'd entered, he dropped from the stage and retreated up the aisle.

"A-a-a-and exit," said Mia as the coach opened the door to the lobby. "Okay, we're down to twenty minutes, people. Move fast."

"Miss Duffy? If you'll permit me?" Mike said.

"What now?" Mia turned on him, waved the clipboard.

"This won't take long," Mike said, and I wondered if everyone heard it too, the sadness in his voice.

Something was going to happen. I could tell. In my head flashed memories of Mike—meeting him on the bench, my audition, the time he sprouted wings and flew, the afternoon we learned to thrust and parry and fall down.

"If I may just say, it's been a pleasure," Mike said. "What I sincerely hope is that all of you continue to value drama, theater, artistic expression in all its forms, continue to let them inspire you and enlarge your understanding of the beautiful world we inhabit for so short a time. As for what's next, here are a few words to live by: The show must go on."

Clive, quick on the uptake, asked, "Yo, Mike, you going somewhere?"

Mia said, "Oh no, you are not. We don't have time."

Mike shook off the sadness, returned to business as usual. I guessed we'd all been wrong. What a relief.

"Speaking of holy spirits," he said, not that anyone had been. "I believe Justin has something to say."

Sure enough, Justin's voice rang out from the speakers above: "We got a little problem."

"No time for problems, Justin," Mia said.

"And the problem is?" Mike asked.

"Mics aren't working. Can't say why."

"I think maybe I can clear this up," Mike said. "Noah—you've got a lavalier, I think?"

Mike held out his hand to take it, fixed me in his gaze, blinked, and just like that I knew he was saying goodbye for real. *No!* I shook my head. *Not now! We need you! I need you!*

He grinned his crooked grin. "'To be, or not to be?'" he spoke into the mic. "How are the levels now, o holy spirit? Any better?"

No answer.

And so Mike began to recite:

> *"You are old, Father William,"* *the young man*
>   *said,*
> *"And your hair has become very white;*
> *And yet you incessantly stand on your head—*
> *Do you think, at your age, it is right?"*

"Oh, wow—how do *you* . . . ," I started to say, but—*thump-squeak*—for the second time that afternoon, the lobby door swung open. It wasn't Fig but my father who walked in, a puzzled expression on his face, one eyebrow raised.

Also, he was pale . . . as if he'd seen a—

"Let's meet our next guest," said Clive.

"Dad? What are you doing here?"

Dad did not answer immediately.

"Professor McNichol?" Marley said. "Are you okay, sir?"

My dad sat down in an aisle seat, shook his head, blinked. "Uh . . . may I ask? Who was that doing the sound check? He almost sounded like my—"

Mia interrupted. "Oh, *fine*. We'll start fifteen minutes late. Everybody, call your parents, and keep in mind it's not my fault. Mike?" She looked around.

We all looked around.

From the booth, the holy spirit spoke. "Sounds good, Mike! Don't know what the trouble was, but I guess it's all cleared up. Ready when you are. Mike? Where'd he go?"

CHAPTER THIRTY-EIGHT

Aghost is not allowed to be seen by anyone who knew him when he was alive.

It was one of the ghostly rules Mike had told me, like how ghosts are called up by a thing called incantation, and how, before they appear the first time, there has to be cold wind.

Now Mike had disappeared a nanosecond before my dad came into the aud.

All at once, I knew the answer to the gin-joint question, and I knew who Mike Einstein was, besides world-famous Broadway director.

Maybe you're way ahead of me.

And if you are, go ahead and add "detecting" to the list of talents I lack.

Dad's color came back, and his eyes regained focus. "I'm fine," he insisted. "A little burp in the space-time continuum is all. Now, where is this director you've been telling me about? I would like to meet him."

Eddie said, "He's gone."

Emma said, "I *told* you he was unreliable."

Madeline said, "Once I had a gerbil that disappeared."

Mia waved her clipboard. "Someone run out and get Fig—Coach Newton, I mean. He'll have to help us. We need someone to get us through tonight and the performance tomorrow—if only to cue Diego from the wings."

"Hey, what are you saying?" Diego said.

Everyone looked at Diego. He wasn't wearing a beret that day, and his scarf was black.

"Not Fig," Fuli said. "He'll shut us down—go straight to Mrs. Winklebottom when he sees the script."

"*And* the ketchup," Brianna said.

I had a bright idea and looked at Dad. "What about Mom? She knows her Shakespeare."

Dad was looking lost again. "I'm not sure I understand. Are you saying your director's gone?"

"Keep up, Dad," I said.

"Your mom has that paper on Emily Dickinson tomorrow," Dad said. "She's up to her eyeballs in hope and feathers."

"What about Miss Magnus?" Marley asked.

"Vacation," I said.

Out of ideas, we looked at one another. Had we come this far only to fail for lack of a grown-up?

"Uh, well . . . ," Dad cleared his throat. "If it's just a matter of someone getting you through tonight and tomorrow, I could, uh . . . possibly do that."

"You hate theater," I said.

"As I've told your mother more than once, 'hate' is too strong a word," Dad said. "Besides, I know the play."

This was true. He had proved it at a dozen Family Dinners.

Clive punched me in the arm, looked at my dad. "You rock, Professor McNichol," he said. "Don't listen to Mr. Pigeon Liver here. Plattsfield-Winklebottom Memorial Sixth-Grade Players, may I introduce our new director!"

Dad took a breath, straightened his shoulders, stood up. "Is there a stage manager?" he asked.

Mia waved her clipboard. "Me, Professor McNichol. Curtain in ten, everybody, so hustle up. The scene is Elsinore."

CHAPTER THIRTY-NINE

If a messy final dress is good luck for the performance, our *Hamlet* was headed for greatness. Still, we did get through it, and around two hours after the curtain rose, I knelt by Fuli's ketchup-covered corpse and said in a loud, clear voice, "'Go, bid the soldiers shoot.'"

At that point, Mike had built in a pause—five, four, three, two, one—so the audience could take in the tragic scene. Then the curtain fell, the dead bodies jumped up, and we all went out to face the audience and take our bows.

Up till now, it had always been Mike in the front row, and Mike's response was always the same. He leaped to his feet, clapped his hands, and shouted: "Riotous applause! Standing O! A triumph!"

Unfortunately, my father did not know the drill, and, instead of applauding, he stared.

Maybe he was affected by the tragedy, I thought. Or maybe it's Sixth-Grade Player PTSD. Whatever it was, the actual performance was twenty-one hours away, and none of us could quit now.

At last Dad rallied, rose from his squeaky seat, tried to smile. "My, my. That was certainly something. Uh . . . I have a few notes."

After which he proceeded to detail every little mistake.

Clive, for example, had forgotten to remove the crown before Claudius bowed his head to pray. The crown fell to the floor, rolled offstage, dropped into the audience, and kept rolling. Since we lacked a spare crown, Mia had been forced to come down out of the wings and crawl on hands and knees to retrieve it.

Likewise, a strand of Ophelia's blond wig had gotten caught on the spade of Gravedigger One, who swung it a little too enthusiastically, tossing the wig into the cheap seats, where as far as any of us knew, it remained.

Yes, I know. I am Gravedigger One.

Then there had been the big duel at the end. Laertes and Hamlet had tangoed away in perfect time, just the way Mike had taught them, till Gertrude stepped backward onto a plastic packet, which exploded in a burst of ketchup all over Claudius's royal-blue tights.

"Does someone in your household have time to do laundry tonight?" Dad had asked Clive.

"I'll do it myself, Professor McNichol," Clive said.

"Good man," said my dad. "And, overall, everyone, perhaps a little more care tomorrow? With head gear and wigs in particular."

Mia checked her watch. "All right, people. Call is for five p.m. tomorrow. Seven o'clock curtain. See you then. Oh, and, people? In memory of Mike: The show will go on!"

"In memory of Mike," Clive said sorrowfully.

"RIP," said Diego.

"I can't help thinking," Madeline said, "that he will be back."

And maybe she was right. With Elsinore in place onstage, the ghost light had moved to the wings. Now, as if responding to a cue, the bulb lit—ready to keep Mike company.

Downstairs in the dressing room we wiped off our makeup, hung up our costumes, said little, did not joke around.

"Good luck with the ketchup stains," I told Clive on our way out.

"Anyway, it'll be over in twenty-four hours," he said, "one way or another."

"That sounds like we're gonna die, Clive, and we're not. Not literally at least."

"Unless Mrs. Winklebottom kills us," Clive said.

Outside, a thin coat of frozen mist, aka ice, clung to the windows and windshield of the car. Dad tossed me the scraper to take care of my side. He used a credit card on his.

In the car, Dad turned on the heater, which blew cold air, and turned the key in the ignition. "Well, that was something, wasn't it?" he said.

I had so much to say, I couldn't answer. It was like the words got stuck. Maybe it was okay to put this conversation off a little longer. Looked at one way, hadn't my family been putting it off for my entire life?

"Noah? You okay?" Dad turned the car out of the school lot.

"Fine," I said. Then, not wanting to sound all teen-rebel rude, I added, "Fine, Dad. Maybe melancholy is all."

"I think the show will be all right, don't you?" Dad asked—hopefully. "Really, it's amazing how much you kids have accomplished. If there are a few, uh . . . miscues tomorrow, the audience will be forgiving."

"You're trying to convince yourself, right?" I said.

"Right," he said.

"Can I ask one thing?" It was one thing among a bunch, and probably the least important. "Why were you so early to pick me up?"

Dad frowned, trying to remember. "Oh yes. Funny, but that seems like a long time ago. I came early because I got a text from the Plattsfield-Winklebottom Memorial Sixth-Grade Players, which—come to think of it—is strange on its own. Do the players have their own wireless account?"

"Not that I ever heard of. What did the text say?" I asked.

"'Rehearsal canceled due to cold weather'— something like that. 'Parents should hasten to retrieve children.'"

"Hasten?"

We were pulling into the garage by this time. Dad turned off the wipers, turned off the ignition, stuffed the keys in his pocket. "Yeah, strange all around. I'll show you the text when we get inside."

"I don't think you're going to find it, Dad."

We got out of the car and made our way into the

mudroom, where I dropped my backpack. We wiped our feet, hung up our coats.

In the kitchen, Dad sat down at the table. "I think I'll just take one more look at the script," he said. "What was it we were talking about?"

"Doesn't matter," I said. "Weird day, huh?"

"Weird day," he agreed. "Oh, and I have a question too. Whose idea was the ketchup?"

CHAPTER FORTY

(*SCENE: 1950s-style kitchen showing little sign of updating. Flurrying snow visible through window over the sink. NOAH and MOM are eating breakfast at a Formica table. DAD, dressed in clothes from the day before, unshaven, bleary-eyed, also seated at the table, writing in a notebook. Several books on Shakespeare and theater are stacked beside him. DAD pours coffee from a carafe into his mug, ladles three spoons of sugar from a sugar bowl. MOM and NOAH watch.*)

MOM: I think you're taking this a little too seriously, dear.

DAD (*doesn't break concentration at first, then realizes he's being watched*): No, no, I don't think so. It's one of the greatest plays ever written, you know. Possibly the greatest.

MOM: I'm more of a *Tempest* girl myself, but that aside, you don't have to do much. Show up. Rally

the players with a pep talk. Look over the props.
Look over the costumes. Keep the set from falling
down.

NOAH: Cue Diego.

MOM: Cue Diego, of course.

NOAH: Basically, Dad, you're backup for Mia.

MOM: What matters now is whatever Mike, the ghost,
did.

NOAH *(surprised, looks at MOM)*: You know he's a
ghost—*was* a ghost?

MOM *(grins, shrugs)*: It's all the talk at Sal's.

NOAH: And at Sal's . . . do people believe it?

MOM *(takes sip of coffee, shrugs)*: I'm not sure about
belief. But everyone loves a good story, even your
father. Earth to Larry McNichol? Dear?

DAD *(once again, after a beat, becomes aware of the silence
and that both MOM and NOAH are looking at him)*:
What? Excuse me, but I'm rather busy. I just want
to be sure I understand Ophelia's motivation in
her scene with Hamlet. Is it love? Or mere infat-
uation?

MOM: Love. Otherwise her drowning is meaningless.
Please feel free to come to me with further questions . . . anytime after my talk on Miss Dickinson,
that is. *(She checks the time on the stovetop clock.)* Okay,

you two. It's a workday if anyone remembers. And I'm due to provide astute analysis of frost images in Emily Dickinson's late poems in fifty-nine minutes and counting. Are you driving, dear?

DAD *(without looking up)*: I'm taking a snow day.

MOM and NOAH *(chorus)*: What?

DAD: Hasn't anyone else looked out the window?

MOM: It's only a *flurry*! The college is open. Don't you have to teach a class . . . ?

DAD: My TA can teach it. She needs the experience. I have a lot to get through to get ready for tonight.

MOM *(raises eyebrows, looks at NOAH, shakes her head)*: I seem to remember *someone* saying that art, theater in particular, is trivial in the face of the challenges we humans face today. I seem to remember *someone* saying only technology can save us, that "all else is folly."

NOAH: Shakespeare?

DAD: Tolstoy. *(He checks clock.)* Look at the time. Noah, get your coat; you'll be late. There's a rule—I looked it up last night—that if you're not in school on the day of an extracurricular, like the Sixth-Grade Play, for example, you can't participate. Whatever happens, we can't risk that.

NOAH *(sighs)*: 'Tis true, 'tis pity, and pity 'tis, 'tis true.

DAD: Act two.

MOM (*rolls eyes, stands up*): Never mind, dear. I'll take him. I've been working on this talk for six months. I have to give it in (*consults clock*) fifty-four minutes, but I see that *you* are much too busy.

CHAPTER FORTY-ONE

Mom and I got in the car. I buckled my seat belt.

"Dad's lost it," I announced.

Mom looked over her shoulder, backed out of the garage. "But in a good cause," she said.

"If he tries to change anything, he'll mess it up. I mean, the dress rehearsal was a mess, but we got through it, and Diego hardly dropped a line." I had jumped into the car so quickly, I hadn't stowed my backpack. It was in my lap. Now I hugged it to me, shifted in my seat.

"I feel your fear," Mom said. "But if Mike has you on firm enough footing, you guys will roll forward like a juggernaut, secure in your own momentum, no force powerful enough to divert you from your course."

"Mom?"

"I'm trying to sound like a physicist. Is it working?"

"No, and please don't," I said. "The world's upside down anyway. Suddenly Dad's all about theater after discouraging me my whole life."

We stopped at a light, the only one between my house and school. Mom looked over. "Can I tell you something?"

"Not if it's mushy-gushy," I said.

Mom laughed. "And what by you is mushy-gushy?"

This I could not possibly explain. Mike's sudden exit the night before—coming at the same moment I realized his identity—had been heartbreaking.

Heartbreaking!

A word that I, a sixth-grade boy in good standing, could not believe I was even capable of thinking. Mike was gone and I would never ask him the questions I'd stored up, never connect with him as my own flesh and blood.

Ha! Funny way to think of a ghost, right?

So, no, Mom, please don't tell me anything else. I can't take it right now.

On the other hand, what if it was important?

"All right, what?" I said.

The light changed. Mom tapped the gas pedal. "Your dad and I met in a theater class. Did you know that? His ambitions were all wrapped up in theater, too, for a while. But his family history"—she shrugged—"anyway, something happened, something tough for him, and it caused him to change course."

I didn't ask what. I didn't want to know. That morning I had too much going on already.

Unfortunately, Mom kept talking. "I think it's been tough for your dad to see you so interested in something that hurt him in the end. I think, if you want to know the truth, he's been trying to protect you. That's what parents do."

We were approaching kid drop-off, known in the afternoon as parent pickup. I saw the bench where I'd first seen Mike, felt a pang. A lot had happened.

"And now he's not protecting me all of a sudden?" I said in spite of myself.

Mom was focused on navigation—cars, kids, parents, crossing guards. She didn't register my question till she had pulled over.

"I don't know why," she said, "but I know how he gets when he's got a challenge. He digs in."

I smiled. "Mike always told us to dig in, too."

"Good advice for a gravedigger," Mom said. "I think I would've liked that Mike. It's a shame he's . . . well, what? Gone? Gone for good? Strange how he disappeared so totally, almost as if he really were a—"

"Don't say it, Mom. And yes, I think you would have liked Mike too. Most of the time you like Dad."

"Some days. But hang on. What was that supposed to—"

My hand was on the latch. I pulled open the door. "See you, Mom. Thanks for the ride! Knock 'em dead with that Emily stuff! You can do it!"

CHAPTER FORTY-TWO

Lunchtime, Monday, May 8, 7 hours till Performance

The snow started falling for real after English.

Then it kept on.

By noon, the irises and daffodils had frozen, and Clive was worried about his apple trees. Any other school district would have called early dismissal, sent us home, but you can't do that in Plattsfield. There'd never be school at all.

That day, Clive, Madeline, Fuli, and I crowded in with the rest of the drama geeks at lunch. Even Eddie Muir sat with us. We were all pretty quiet. We had plenty to worry about. Our director had disappeared. His replacement was a rookie. The show we were about to stage was not the one either Fig or Mrs. Winklebottom, or most of the parents, were expecting.

238

Mia said, "On Monday, we will all have detention."

Eddie said, "For the rest of the school year."

Brianna said, "For the rest of our *lives!*"

"Maybe the snow is, like, a good thing?" Lila said. "Maybe no one will, like, even show up."

"Oh, they'll show up," Sarah said. "This is the North Country. People will tromp here by snowshoe or snowplow."

"How's your dad doing?" Marley asked me.

"He's lost it," I said.

Fuli said, "Perhaps that is a good thing as well. He will have empathy. Many of the characters in the play lose it: Hamlet, Ophelia, Gertrude, the ghost . . ."

"Basically, everybody *except* Polonius," Emma said.

"And Fortinbras," I put in.

Emma wasn't sitting next to me that day. In fact, thinking about it, she hadn't seemed so super friendly lately. At first when I had found out she liked me, or people said so anyway, I thought it was weird, and then I thought it was gross. I mean, Emma who had an underactive imagination? Emma who was always bragging about her parents and their money?

Emma who called Clive and me dumb because we believed Mike was a ghost?

But then I thought some more, how maybe she

was just trying to get my attention like people said. If that was true, should I be flattered? So even though Emma wasn't the kind of person I could ever see myself liking, at least she was a person with the good taste to like me.

Right?

Mia looked at her. "So, Emma, now you're okay being Polonius?"

Emma glared at Diego. Apparently she hadn't forgiven him yet, or anyway she didn't see the PicPoc as an homage. Diego shrugged and smiled back shyly. "You know I'm sorry, right? I didn't mean to hurt your feelings."

Emma ignored him. "I like Mike's *interpretation* of Polonius. I like that *Mike* thought Polonius was sane and happy."

Marley said, "I miss Mike."

Clive said, "We all miss Mike, I think."

Madeline said, "I miss my gerbil, too."

CHAPTER FORTY-THREE

5:30 p.m., Monday, May 8, Countdown to Performance: 90 minutes

Snow or no, all us Sixth-Grade Players arrived early in the dressing rooms below the aud—all except Eddie, who played the ghost, Guilden-stern, and Osric.

Where was he, anyway?

If there's one thing Plattsfield parentals are good at, it's driving their vehicles in snow. Still, it was possible his family's car had gotten stuck.

He'd show up eventually; he had to.

Clive and I helped each other with costumes and makeup. For my first character, Marcellus, I wore a helmet that looked like an upside-down mixing bowl, a gray tunic over black pants, and boots that looked lace-up but were actually Velcro.

The pants and boots I wore for the whole show.

The mixing bowl got changed out depending on my character. In the final scene, it was a crown.

Getting ready, all of us guys were pretty quiet but for Diego. If Diego had been quiet, I would have worried he was dead. He poked and pinched and pretended to rip costumes. He hid Claudius's eyebrow pencil. For Diego, this could've been any day of the week, any random rehearsal at which he'd probably forget Horatio's lines and trip over a headstone and skewer himself with a rapier, not that he cared.

"Is your heart pounding?" I asked Clive.

"It pounds when I look at myself in the mirror. Yikes. I am *ba-a-a-a-ad!*"

This was true. Claudius's evil eyebrows slanted north to south, temple to nose, and he had a dusting of powder on his hair to show that he was old-old-old. His costume was white, which Mike called ironic since the guy in white usually is the good guy. But since Hamlet, the broody one in mourning for his father, wore black, the villain's white was supposed to show contrast.

The minutes ticked down. Still no Eddie. Did I mention his character comes on early in act one?

What were we supposed to do without him?

I picked up my phone, called him for about the tenth time.

Everyone else had called or texted too.

The messages showed delivered, but he wasn't picking up.

Clipboard in one hand, stopwatch in the other, Mia appeared in the doorway. She was wearing a headset so she could communicate with Justin in the tech booth.

"Five minutes, everybody. Stand by for act one curtain. Stand by."

"What are we going to do about Eddie?" Clive asked.

Mia's face looked the same as usual but for the line between her brows. It was always there but now it looked more like a canyon. "Noah's dad will go on as the ghost if necessary. His face is hidden under his helmet. No one will know."

"Dad doesn't know the part!" I squawked.

"You'd be surprised," Mia said. "Four minutes, you guys. Better get your butts upstairs."

Should I have worried? Probably. But I had my own stuff to worry about, like digging in, inhabiting my character, or—failing that—at least remembering my lines.

Clive, Diego, and I fell in behind the girls, climbed the stairs, crossed the fluorescent-lit hallway, opened the heavy metal door, passed through it, climbed three more steps, came out into the dimly lit backstage.

You might've expected excitement to make us giggle, shove one another, tug one another's costumes, generally fool around; in reality we were so far beyond that, even Diego, that we stayed absolutely quiet.

Meanwhile, from the house came the sound of footfalls, squeaky seats, chatting, and laughing. Waiting in the wings, I wished I were in the audience too, with nothing to do but sit and watch and criticize every tiny mistake.

Wait! No! No way to think!

My mom was out there rooting for me, and Clive's parents, and Brianna's relatives from Poughkeepsie, and Coach Fig's family, and Coach Fig himself, if he'd recovered enough from the wedding cancelation.

Mrs. Winklebottom would be out there, too.

Detention forever.

Don't think about that!

But what if she realized the script had changed, leaped from her seat hollering because the wholesome families of Plattsfield should not be subjected to so much blood, even if it was artistic?

If only Mike were here. He could have taken care of her. He wouldn't even have needed lightning or swordplay, just a sudden silencing case of laryngitis.

Dad might know about lasers, but laryngitis he could never pull off.

"Thirty seconds, everybody," Mia said. "Places for act one. The scene is . . . *Elsinore.*"

Since Claudius didn't come on till scene two, Clive's responsibility was to hand me my sword, look me over, make sure no boogers had escaped my nose, no ketchup stained my doublet. Apparently, I was okay. Clive nodded approval.

"'If it be not now, yet it will come'," he whispered.

"'Readiness is all,'" I said. "Act five."

With the curtain between us and the audience, Brianna, Diego, and I walked out onstage. At the same time, I spotted him out of the corner of my eye—our ghost. *Phew!* Eddie must have made it after all.

"Standby for entrance, Mr. Muir," Mia said calmly. "And it's a good thing you're dead, because other-wise I'd kill you."

So there I stood downstage right on the ramparts of Elsinore.

I forgot my dad and Mrs. Winklebottom and the snow outside and how our ghost had been late. I forgot about the rustling, fidgeting, giggling audience on the other side of the curtain. I forgot about Mike. I dug in and inhabited my character, who was about to tell Hamlet's best friend, Horatio, that he'd seen something strange hovering around the castle, and what exactly did Horatio want to do about it?

"A-a-a-nd, curtain," said Mia, causing Clive and Sarah to pull the ropes at the same time that—*bzz*— the holy spirit brought up the lights.

When the audience was done gasping and murmuring at our beautiful Elsinore, Brianna took a breath and spoke: "'Sit down awhile, and let us once again assail your ears, that are so fortified against our story, what we have two nights seen.'"

CHAPTER FORTY-FOUR

A little more than two hours later, Hamlet and Laertes lay spattered in ketchup, the poisoned bodies of Gertrude and Claudius beside them.

"'Good night, sweet prince,'" Horatio said, "'and flights of angels sing thee to thy rest.'"

After that there were a few more speeches and then, the real highlight, Fortinbras spoke the last line: "'Go, bid the soldiers shoot.'"

Five, four, three, two, one. The lights went black. In the wings, my dad and Mia brought down the curtain.

"Places for the curtain call, everyone. Places!" Mia said.

Hamlet, Laertes, Gertrude, and Claudius jumped to their feet. All of us scurried into the wings. We were giddy, full of ourselves, delighted. *We had done it!*

Except . . .

. . . all at once and all together, we came to a realization.

There was no sound from the house.

No cheering. No applause. No nothing,

For all we could tell, the audience had gotten up and left.

Even my mom? She couldn't stick around and clap a little?

But we had worked so hard!

Oh sure, there had been a few muffed moments. Polonius had gotten tangled in the arras, Gertrude had slipped in ketchup, I had almost fallen into Ophelia's grave, and Diego—I swore I would punch the kid—sailed through the "flesh" part fine but giggled when Laertes said "virgin."

All in all, though, the performance had gone well, way better than the final dress. When Hamlet said, "To be, or not to be," the house was quiet as, well, a tomb. When Sarah as Gertrude delivered the speech about how Ophelia died, "There is a willow grows aslant a brook . . . ," I heard sniffles and sobs from the audience. I even felt a tear in my eye myself.

But now, lining up for the curtain call, we gave one another worried sidelong looks. One more time,

Dad and Mia put their hands on the ropes, ready to raise the curtain, and then, finally, I heard a smatter of applause.

Moms, I thought. At least a few moms were still there.

The curtain rose. The cast had nowhere to hide, not even behind our characters. We faced friends and families as ourselves. The audience hadn't left, it turned out. They were there, staring back at us, but they didn't look hostile.

What they looked was more in shock.

And then I remembered the obvious. They had expected a *Lion King* ending. What they got was spilled ketchup and corpses.

Still, we had rehearsed this curtain call. And we would darned well *do* this curtain call. Just like in rehearsal, Eddie Muir, Brianna, and I—the minor characters—stepped forward into the silence and bowed, feeling, if I may speak for myself, queasy.

And that's when it happened. Like a rockslide starting with pebbles, or an avalanche with a few flakes of snow, the faint sound grew louder until, seconds later, it became a roar, and every single person in the audience leaped to their feet.

And what's more . . .

. . . the absolute first person to leap, which I know because she was in the front row directly opposite me, was Mrs. Winklebottom herself. Beside her, and—wait one second, wasn't she supposed to be on vacation?—was Miss Magnus.

Both of them were crying.

"Bravo!" "Bravo!" "Bravo!" came shouts from throughout the aud.

It was just the way Mike had predicted: Riotous applause! Standing O! *Plattsfield-Winklebottom Memorial Sixth-Grade Players triumph!*

CHAPTER FORTY-FIVE

ownstairs, we high-fived each other, poked, prodded, made noise, made rude jokes—the usual sixth-grade stuff. In other words, we returned to being ourselves, except a super-happy, super-proud version of ourselves.

We had done it!

I was so happy I even looked over at Emma, ready to smile, ready to think of her as an okay person who was allowed to *like* me if she wanted. But Emma wasn't paying attention. She was smiling like Hanukkah at Diego. And he was smiling back.

A few minutes later, Clive and I were sitting at the mirror, wiping off our makeup when Dad checked in, told us we were fantastic.

"When Eddie was so late?" he said. "I thought we were done for! But that kid who filled in at the last minute was amazing. Who was he, anyway?"

I didn't know what Dad was talking about, and I didn't have time to wonder because someone squealed from the aud stage above us.

"Want to see what's going on up there?" Clive asked. "Come on, Professor McNichol."

Down the hall, up the stairs, through the door to the stage, and there, in the wings, was Mia, source of the squeal. Before her, the stage was bare except for fifteen folding chairs.

Elsinore—graveyard, parapets, chapel, arras, and all—had disappeared.

The cast party was scheduled for the next afternoon. The parents said it was so we kids could get our sleep, but it was really so they could get theirs. Parents were invited to the cast party, too.

The plan was potluck in the caf.

Yawn.

But then—more help from supernatural forces?

On Saturday morning, Coach Fig sent an email announcing that the venue (useful word!) had changed. It was now a swanky lake-view lodge.

There would be a DJ! Excellent food! Flowers and a ginormous cake!

There would be champagne for the parents and pineapple in the fruit salad!

How had such a thing happened?

Maybe you're ahead of me this time, too.

Coach Newton, wedding planner, had tried to cancel arrangements for the wedding of the century. But the baker, the florist, the caterer, the DJ—they all told him the same thing. Payment had been made in full the day before. Wedding or no wedding, the party must go on!

In which case, why not make it *our* party?

The lodge was all wood and glass, with a stone fireplace and floor-to-ceiling views of snow-covered trees, the glittering lake, and beyond it the shores of Vermont, the undiscovered country.

JK. Even I have been to Vermont. So—I checked—has Fuli.

Not that I was super focused on scenery. Instead my eyes were glued to the buffet: crunchy fried things, cheesy biscuits, mini pizzas dotted (so sad) with clams, all sorts of sweet and salty things, ridiculous amounts of bacon.

If only there'd been dumplings from Himalaya, it would've been perfect.

Sampling it all kept me so busy I forgot about asking Eddie why he'd been late to the performance.

Until I remembered. Snow, right?

"No, not snow," said Eddie between bites. He was standing next to Clive on the other side of the punch bowl. "Only my unreliable parents. They got mixed up about which one was supposed to drive me. I was freaking out till I got a text that said my understudy could go on as the ghost. I just had to make it in time for Guildenstern."

"We don't have understudies," I said.

"That's what I thought. But someone went on for me," Eddie said.

"So"—I tried to put it together, looked at Clive— "we still don't know who played the ghost?"

"He was tall like Eddie," Clive said, "and really convincing the way he glided around and . . . Oh."

"Oh," I echoed as the obvious explanation came to me. "Because it wasn't my dad, and it wasn't Mia, and there's only one other, uh . . . *person* I can think of who knows the part. Knew the part."

Diego was really stylin' that day: bright pink beret, lime-green scarf. With advice from Emma, he'd spent the whole party snapping photos of the food, the views, everybody. Would the next immortal PW

PicPoc be #CastParty? Now he said, "Heck yeah!" and looked around like he wanted to snap a picture of a ghost.

But we all knew that was impossible.

CHAPTER FORTY-SIX

(SCENE: Living room of the McNichol household, early evening. Entryway is downstage left, stairs to second floor stage right. Center stage are a sofa and coffee table, both well worn and comfortable. NOAH and DAD are seated on the sofa, cozy in lamplight, looking at an old black leather scrapbook.)

NOAH: So your dad used to read you "Father William" at bedtime, same as you used to read it to me.

DAD *(nods)*: One of my few memories of him—that is, the few memories besides what I saw in the paper when I was old enough to read. Clippings like these. *(He points, flips pages.)* Oh, one more memory.

NOAH: What?

DAD: The birthday when he gave me the poster, the signed one from *Star Wars* you have in your bedroom? Alec Guinness as Obi-Wan Kenobi. My father knew a lot of actors.

NOAH: So your dad was almost never around, and you were mad at him for that.

DAD: I got over it.

(Beat, NOAH looks up at DAD, as in, Seriously, DAD?)

DAD *(smiles sheepishly)*: Or maybe I didn't. My father— my biological father—was a big deal. I admired him and I envied him. Meanwhile, I was a lonely little boy left home with a nanny.

NOAH *(wide-eyed)*: That's the saddest thing I ever heard!

DAD: Oh, now. There are plenty of sadder things, and don't get me wrong. For a long time all I wanted was to be like my dad. In high school, I was a drama geek too.

NOAH: That's why you know your Shakespeare.

DAD *(nods)*: And in college I directed a production of *Macbeth*. My parents had been divorced forever by that time. I hardly ever saw my father, but I invited him to opening night.

NOAH: And?

DAD *(shrugs)*: He didn't show.

NOAH *(winces)*: That's terrible.

DAD *(nods, sighs)*: Yeah, it was. He sent a note the next

day. He was on his third wife by that time. He said he was sorry and so on, promised to come next time. But there was no next time. I went a different direction. Happily, Bill McNichol had adopted me when he married my mom, so I no longer had the family name. It would have been awkward to be a physicist named Einstein.

NOAH: Then Mike, your dad, died in 2014.

DAD *(nods)*: It was sudden. I hadn't seen him in years. By then it shouldn't have mattered. But it did. *(He looks at NOAH.)* You don't remember. You were only a little guy. But it was a gloomy time for me. He was gone, and he'd never make it right.

NOAH *(eagerly)*: But, Dad—now he did. He went to all the trouble to come back as a ghost and fix things.

DAD: Noah . . . there's no such thing as—

NOAH: Listen, Dad. Here is how it went down. I recited, "You are old, Father William," and he heard me, and he came. This *(he points to photo in the album)* is Mike. All of us Sixth-Grade Players saw him. Physics doesn't explain everything, Dad, or at least it doesn't yet.

DAD: "There are more things in heaven and earth?"

NOAH: And Mike fixed a lot. You like theater again.

I know a lot more about it than I used to. You told me the truth about your family. Mike even fixed Mrs. Winklebottom.

DAD: What?

NOAH: At the party yesterday, she said the show convinced her No-Trauma Drama is a mistake, that kids can handle real art. Miss Magnus is really happy about that.

DAD: I thought you told me Miss Magnus would be on vacation for the performance?

NOAH: In the end, she couldn't stand to leave. She was just too curious. *(He nods toward the book, flips pages.)* Look at the shows Mike did, the awards he won!

DAD *(shrugs)*: You will note there are no awards in here for parenting.

NOAH *(shut down, hesitates)*: You know, Dad, Shakespeare has something to say about that too. Hamlet's talking about his father. He was great, a legend, a king—but he wasn't perfect.

DAD: "He was a man. Take him for all in all."

NOAH and DAD *(together)*: Act one.

NOAH *(flips to the last page in the book)*: Hey, look at this program. *(He reads.)* "The Plattsfield-Winklebottom Memorial Sixth-Grade Players present William Shakespeare's *Hamlet,* one night only, directed by Mike Einstein and Larry McNichol. Featuring Mike Einstein himself as the Ghost."

DAD *(trying not to hyperventilate)*: My mother brought this album from Florida at Passover. Did you paste that program in there? But you couldn't have known Eddie wouldn't play the ghost, or that I—

NOAH *(shaking his head)*: I'm not the only funny guy in the family, Dad. Do you still think there's no such thing as ghosts?

DAD *(looks up from scrapbook, looks at NOAH)*: I don't know what to think.

NOAH: He's still here. *(He looks around.)* Maybe it's true that our ghosts are always among us.

DAD: Is that Shakespeare?

NOAH: Nope, not this time. This time it is I, Noah McNichol.